"LET'S GO WALK THE PATH."

"No!" Charlotte cried out. And then she said, "I mean, not now. It's getting too dark." She pointed. "In the center . . . that's where I was when it happened. The Disappearance. I was in the center."

"Where were the others?" Jake asked.

She didn't answer.

Cam spoke. "Charlotte? Where are the others?"

After another few seconds, Charlotte spoke.

"There are no others."

Other Avon Books in the
LAST ON EARTH *Trilogy*
by Marilyn Kaye

Avon Books are available at special quantity discounts for bulk purchases for sales promotions, premiums, fund raising or educational use. Special books, or book excerpts, can also be created to fit specific needs.

For details write or telephone the office of the Director of Special Markets, Avon Books, Inc., Dept. FP, 1350 Avenue of the Americas, New York, New York 10019, 1-800-238-0658.

LAST ON EARTH

BOOK THREE:

THE

RETURN

MARILYN KAYE

AVON BOOKS NEW YORK

AVON BOOKS, INC.
1350 Avenue of the Americas
New York, New York 10019

Copyright © 1999 by Marilyn Kaye
Published by arrangement with the author
Visit our website at http://www.AvonBooks.com
Library of Congress Catalog Card Number: 98-93052
ISBN: 0-380-79834-4

First Avon Books Printing: February 1999

AVON TRADEMARK REG. U.S. PAT. OFF. AND IN OTHER COUNTRIES, MARCA REGISTRADA, HECHO EN U.S.A.

Printed in the U.S.A.

WCD 10 9 8 7 6 5 4 3 2 1

For Valérie and Eric Huybrechts,
Charlotte and Jeanne

THE

RETURN

one

the flight had been calm for over an hour. Maybe that was why the sudden brief shudder produced a muffled scream from the rear. Jake looked over his shoulder at the frightened girl who was gripping the hand of an unsmiling boy.

"You okay, Shalini?"

Alex answered for her. "First time on a plane." His expression made it clear that they didn't want to be bothered, so Jake turned to the girl who sat next to him.

He knew for a fact that this wasn't *her* first plane ride. Ashley had been an almost supermodel in her former life, and she'd flown all over the world for fashion shows and photo shoots. A little turbulence wouldn't bother her. In fact, she had slept right through it.

Now the plane was steady again. Jake addressed the passenger across the aisle. "Looks like Travis really knows how to handle a plane."

The small, pale boy didn't look up from his laptop.

"Cam?"

With a show of reluctance, the boy tore his eyes from the screen. "What?"

"I was just saying, Travis didn't lie about knowing how to fly a plane."

Cam nodded and turned back to his computer.

Jake shifted restlessly in his seat. He'd flown before, many times. Every summer, before it happened, he and his family flew to Florida to have a vacation with his grandparents at their condo in Boca Raton. But he'd never had to sit still for this long before. How long was a flight to California anyway? Five hours? Or would it take longer in a small plane like this?

He was bored. He tried again to start a conversation with Cam. "What are you doing?"

It was a moment before Cam replied. "Checking out the chat rooms on the West Coast."

"Find anyone?"

"No, not yet."

"You hear from the group in Los Angeles again?"

"Yeah, they're meeting us at LAX."

"What's LAX?"

"The airport."

"Oh." Jake stretched his neck to get a look at Cam's screen. "Hey, how did you get on-line? There's no phone on this plane, is there?"

"Remote," Cam replied shortly.

"Huh?"

"It's a remote device, like a cordless phone. It's too complicated to explain."

Jake didn't take offense at the comment. They all acknowledged Cam as the only one among them who was truly computer literate and understood the intricacies of technology. As long as he took care of that, his social inadequacies were excused.

Funny, Jake had always thought of himself as pretty inadequate in that regard. Before, back in the senior class at Madison High, he was considered something of a loner. He'd tried not to get too involved in other people's lives. Now, with only twenty-five people left on Earth to communicate with, he'd somehow become a leader.

But apparently, at this moment, no one seemed to be in need of a leader's companionship. Gazing around, he saw Kesha with her eyes closed, apparently sleeping. In front of her, Martina was engaged in what appeared to be a very private conversation with David. Interesting, given the fact that Martina hated David's guts for having broken the heart of her twin sister, Rosa, just last summer.

Jake had to smile at himself. Just a couple of months ago, he wouldn't have been privy to gossip like that. Now they all seemed to know everything about one another.

So . . . Alex, Shalini, Cam, Kesha, Martina, David, Ashley . . . who was left? Donna had to be up front in the cockpit, taking great pride in the fact that her boyfriend was flying the plane. Jake was forced to return to the mode of communication he'd relied on before he became, for better or worse, a leader of a small group of survivors.

He pulled out his journal from his backpack and opened it to the last entry, composed just a couple of hours ago.

So now we're on our way to California to meet with this group who survived the Disappearance. At least we can be pretty sure they'll be on our side, and we have an idea of what we're up against. Sort of.

Beside him, Ashley stirred. As he looked at her beautiful face, she opened her eyes and smiled. "Hi," she murmured.

"Hi," he replied. "Hungry?"

"No. Thirsty." She snuggled against his shoulder. "Ring for the flight attendant and get me a Diet Coke."

"Very funny," Jake replied. His hand caressed the soft fuzz on her head. "Your hair's growing."

"Mm," she said drowsily. "That's what hair does." Then she was asleep again.

With a sigh, Jake went back to his journal.

I'm trying to imagine what the rest are doing back at the Community. Getting nuts, probably. Travis was the only element holding them together, keeping them relatively normal.

As much as he'd disliked Travis's form of totalitarian government, it had kept the party animals in check. He recalled their first night together, just hours after they had emerged from a classroom to find that the rest of the world had vanished. Even in their state of shock, some of them had started to party. By now, they were probably engaged in a nonstop orgy of sex, drugs, and rock and roll. Of the fifteen kids who had stayed behind in New York, not one of them had any real leadership qualities in Jake's opinion. After the Disappearance—D-day, as they called it now—Travis, as senior class president, had automatically been handed the role of presiding over the twenty-five survivors.

Jake didn't have any problem with this at the time. He'd certainly had no aspirations to lead the group himself. But when Travis'd turned into a dictator and refused to consider the possibility that the world they'd known was not past recovery, Jake had been pressured into leading an alternative group on a mission to discover what really happened.

And now they knew—sort of. There had been communication—electronically, telepathicly, and through a dream. At least, they could assume that the population of the world, the citizens of Earth, were still in existence—in some other place. In some other form.

As for Travis—he was with them, now. Jake kept telling himself that was good. The more the merrier, safety in numbers, united we stand, and all that. But in the back of his mind, a question remained, and it itched him like a mosquito bite. Who was their real leader?

He didn't want to think about this now, so he returned to the journal and tried to think of something new and original to write.

I wonder what these guys in California are like. It's weird. We're just getting used to thinking of ourselves as the last on Earth, and it turns out we're not. Cam hasn't found out too much about them. We have no idea how many of them there are. We don't know why they survived. Of course, we don't know why we survived either. They probably don't know any more than we do.

He read his words over. Then he added, *Or maybe they do.* And how would that affect the balance of power? he wondered.

He frowned. Why was he torturing himself with questions he couldn't possibly answer? He needed to take a minute to count his blessings.

He was alive. He was whole and intact and he still had his feet firmly planted on planet Earth. Well, figuratively speaking, he amended as he glanced out the window at the clouds floating beneath them. Most important, the person he loved was alive, whole, and sitting beside him.

As if on cue, Ashley opened her eyes. "Hello again," he said.

She straightened up in her seat. "How long was I sleeping?" she asked.

"Long enough for me to miss you," he said in his deepest, most poetic voice.

She grinned. "Oh, that's excellent. Keep talking that way and I just might think you're coming on to me."

"And you just might be right," he said.

Ashley laughed out loud. "We sound like a very stupid teen movie," she pointed out to him.

"That's because we're two very stupid teens," he replied.

She punched him lightly. "Speak for yourself." She stretched and moved her head from side to side as if to shake the sleep out. "I had the most amazing dream. It was so real."

"About what?"

"Corey."

That wasn't the answer he wanted to hear, but he went along with it. "What about Corey?"

"The usual. I could see him, I could hear his voice. In the dream, I was trying to let him know we're coming to save him, but he couldn't hear me. Just like the other times."

"Of course, this time was just a dream," Jake noted. "It wasn't like before, when you were having those visions on TV."

"It seemed just as real," Ashley said thoughtfully. "And if he can get inside my television set, why wouldn't he be able to get inside my head?"

Jake didn't reply. He couldn't say he was crazy about the idea of another man inside Ashley's head. But Ashley went on talking, not sensing his discomfort.

"Corey's an incredible person, Jake. If anyone could get into my head, he could. I can't wait for you to know him."

Jake had already heard many, many times about the kind of person Corey was. He knew that the fashion photographer had been a special and protective friend to Ashley. In the past weeks, she'd had recurring dreams about him, and then his image had appeared to her on a TV screen.

"You never saw anyone else in those TV visions, did you?" he asked her. "Like your mother, for example. She must be there, too, wherever Corey is."

"No, but she doesn't have Corey's spiritual strength, his ability to connect," Ashley told him. "She could barely get through to me when we were standing side by side! Corey . . . it was like, he *knew* me, better than I knew myself. We had this bond, you know? He could see beyond all the hype and the glamour and all that supermodel crap. He knew what was real. I could communicate with Corey in a way I'd never communicated with anyone in my life.''

She didn't add ''until I met you.'' He tried not to accept the twinge of jealousy that tugged at his heart, but it was there. That little green-eyed monster had taken up permanent residence.

Ashley had assured him that her relationship with Corey had never been romantic. From what Jake understood, Corey had been more of a father figure, a big brother, something like that. In his mind, he envisioned a much older man, balding and paunchy, with a jovial Santa Claus air. Or maybe he was young and handsome, but effeminate, flamboyant, and probably gay. Certainly not the kind of guy Jake would ever consider to be a threat.

But even so, the idea that anyone else—young, old, gay, straight, male or female—could be closer to Ashley than he was . . .

Suddenly, the plane lurched. There was a familiar squeal from the rear. Then the plane began to bounce, hard, and even the more experienced fliers began to take notice.

Ashley slipped her hand into Jake's. ''I hate this,'' she murmured.

''It's just an air pocket,'' Jake said, but his own stomach was flip-flopping as the plane continued to bounce. It felt like they were riding in an old car and there were massive potholes on the road.

The plane dropped, and now even Cam looked up from his computer. Jake shifted in his seat, and he saw that Shalini was sobbing softly and Alex was deathly pale. The plane plunged again—a thousand feet? Two thousand feet? Martina had a rosary in her hand and her lips were moving. Even Kesha, who prided herself on her strength and composure and lack of fear, was gripping the armrests of her seat so tightly that her knuckles had turned white.

Jake knew he should do something, say something, try to calm them all down. But he was scared, too, and he didn't know what to say. Now the plane was rocking back and forth, like a tiny flimsy boat on an immense, angry sea.

Through an intercom, the disembodied voice of their pilot cut the tension. "Sorry, folks. I couldn't talk to you sooner because I was trying to navigate us out of this turbulence. It looks like we're going to have a few more minutes of this. In these small planes, you feel everything. But there's nothing to worry about—it's all normal, and everything's fine up here. So take a deep breath try to relax, and I'll get us through it as quickly as I can."

Travis's calm voice had the effect of a verbal tranquilizer. Jake could hear the sighs of relief as everyone released fear and tension. And Travis was true to his word. Within minutes, the turbulence disappeared.

Donna appeared from behind the curtain. "Is everyone okay?" she asked anxiously.

There was a general murmur of assent. Donna smiled happily, her eyes shining with pride. "Isn't he wonderful?" she asked simply. Then she disappeared back behind the curtain.

Ashley was smiling. "Now, *that's* the face of a woman in love."

Jake turned to her. "Is *this* the face of a woman in love?"

Ashley rolled her eyes. "Oh, Jake, have a little faith."

She was right. Why did he have to be so damned insecure? Ashley loved him as much as he loved her, and he had to stop questioning it.

Love wasn't the only thing that made him feel insecure. Travis . . . just now he'd sounded really good, totally confident and in control. And everyone seemed to take comfort in his words and to believe them. They were trusting him with their lives. Which was as it should be, Jake supposed. Didn't people always want to trust the pilot of their plane?

But he couldn't help wondering if this trust would extend beyond their flight to California. Which, in Jake's opinion, was *not* as it should be.

Kesha tried to be discreet as she let out her breath once the plane became steady again. She didn't want her fear to be apparent to the others. And she certainly didn't want anyone to think that the cessation of her fear had anything to do with Travis.

She really had to let go of that old rivalry. Just because Travis had beaten her in the election for senior class president last spring was no reason to hold a grudge, especially given their current circumstances. That would be just too juvenile, especially for someone like Kesha Greene. Kesha Greene had a reputation. She hoped nobody had noticed how scared she was. Were they all talking about her now?

She leaned back in her seat and allowed herself

to eavesdrop surreptitiously on the conversation going on in the seats behind her.

David Chu, the Don Juan of Madison High, was speaking. "Look, Martina, I didn't want to hurt Rosa. I just wasn't ready to make a commitment."

"Did you tell her you loved her?" Martina wanted to know.

"Maybe," David allowed. "Probably. Yeah, sure, I said that. But it doesn't mean anything."

"It meant something to Rosa."

"Yeah, well . . . I didn't know she was taking it so seriously."

"Did she mean anything to you at all?"

"Of course she did!"

At that point, Kesha took out the Walkman she'd brought and firmly clamped the earphones to her ears. She hit the Play button and let the happy reggae rhythms block out any further conversation.

That exchange between Martina and David . . . it was not only uninteresting, it was incomprehensible. She couldn't understand how or why any woman could fall in love with David Chu. Okay, in all objectivity, she had to acknowledge that he was incredibly handsome in a conventional sort of way. But he was also shallow, superficial, and as far as she could tell, intellectually limited. Not to mention morally and ethically challenged.

She hadn't really known Rosa, except for a brief time when her spirit had taken over Martina's body back in Central Park. But she knew Martina, and since she and Rosa were identical twins, Kesha had to assume the sisters were similar in nature. She couldn't imagine someone as smart as Martina falling for a guy like David.

She tilted her seat back. Now she had a glimpse of Shalini and Alex. What a pair *they* made. Alex was your basic leather-jacket rebel without a cause, the son of Russian immigrants. Shalini was the shy, demure daughter of traditional Indian parents who still believed in male domination and arranged marriages. What could those two possibly have in common?

Then there was Travis and Donna. That was the most difficult relationship in the world for her to understand. Donna was her best friend—they'd been pals for years. How she could fall madly in love with a plastic political beast like Travis was beyond Kesha.

But then, most of the relationships she observed were beyond her comprehension. Jet-set supermodel Ashley and moody Jake from Queens—where did that came from?

It dawned on her that the only other person sitting alone on the plane was Cam. But that wasn't surprising. Cam was a tekkie, a nerd, a computer junkie whose socks never matched. People like Cam were never in couples.

And what about people like her? She'd always been reasonably popular, she'd always had friends. But she'd never been in love, and no one had ever been in love with her. It never used to bother her much. She figured she'd meet Mr. Right someday. He'd be strong, determined—a brother, of course—someone who wouldn't be intimidated or put off by an energetic, assertive young woman who refused to conform to stereotypes of femininity. She thought she'd find him in college or out in the real world. Maybe they'd be working side by side in the inner city.

She couldn't count on that anymore. As far as she knew, at the moment there were only thirteen potential Mr. Rights on the face of the Earth, and none of them came close to her ideal. To be honest, she knew she wasn't their ideal either. Maybe in California . . .

Her thoughts were disturbed by Travis's voice. "We'll be landing in about twenty minutes," he intoned. "Please put your seat backs in upright positions, return tray tables, and fasten your seat belts."

Pompous ass, Kesha thought. If they weren't landing for twenty minutes, why did they have to put themselves in landing position *now*?

People were responding. Across the aisle, she saw Martina take out a compact and check herself in the mirror. She could hear Cam closing his computer. But there was no expectant buzz or sense of anticipation in the cabin. The silence was heavy.

Kesha broke it. "How many people are going to be there?"

"I don't know," Cam replied. "The person I've been e-mailing with, he never said."

"He? You know it's a he?"

"No," Cam acknowledged. "I don't know anything about him. Or her."

"Or it." That came from Alex.

"What do you mean 'it'?" Jake asked.

"How do we know this isn't some kind of scam?" Alex fired back. "We could be walking into an alien trap."

Martina spoke. "If aliens had been communicating with Cam, they wouldn't need to lure us to Los Angeles. They could have taken us from wherever we were, just like they took everyone else.''

"Yeah, well, whatever," Alex said. "All I know is, we're landing in Los Angeles, we're totally defenseless, and we don't know what's waiting for us.''

"You got another option?" Martina asked.

Jake joined in the discussion. "Yeah, instead of complaining, why don't you present an idea, Alex?''

"Because none of you want to hear my ideas,'' Alex shot back.

"Because your ideas always suck,'' David said.

"Would you all please shut up!" Ashley burst out. "I'm feeling nervous enough already.''

Maybe she had good reason to be, Kesha thought as the plane began its descent. Maybe they all did.

two

they all saw the bus at the same time. It would have been impossible to miss it. Parked at the end of the runway, it stood out in contrast to the dull silver and gray of the small planes strewn around the landing field.

Jake thought it had to have been an ordinary school bus at one time. He could still make out the familiar yellow, now a background to bright splashes of color that seemed to have been more recently applied.

"It looks like something from the sixties," Martina murmured, and Jake agreed. The bus was decorated with large, crudely painted flowers, signs of the zodiac, and a peace symbol. There were graffiti, too—words like "love" and "harmony" added to the overall psychedelic feel. At any moment, Jake half expected to see a crew of long-haired hippies pour out of the vehicle singing "Age of Aquarius."

But when the door of the bus swung open, only one person emerged. Of the group that had come off the plane and now stood blinking on the runway, no one moved. They just stood there and gawked. It was rude, of course, but Jake couldn't blame them. It had been a while since they'd seen a person they couldn't recognize.

Her blond hair was pulled away from her face and hung in one long French braid down her back. Her smiling face was open and friendly, and there was a sprinkling of freckles across her upturned nose. She wore baggy overalls, which were rolled up at the ankles, and a baseball cap was perched precariously on her head.

"At least she's not wearing love beads," Ashley murmured.

"Do you think we could have passed through a time warp or something?" Martina asked uneasily.

The girl on the bus steps didn't appear to be alarmed by *their* appearance. "Hi," she announced. "Welcome to sunny California. I'm Charlotte."

Travis was the first to recover his social graces. He stepped out of the group and moved toward Charlotte with an air of assurance. "Hello, Charlotte. Thank you for your welcome. Excuse us for staring, but—"

She interrupted his greeting. "Are you Cam?" she asked eagerly.

"No, that's me." Cam came forward with his right hand extended. Charlotte clambered down the steps and flung her arms around him.

"Cam, I'm so happy to actually see you in person! I feel like I already know you after all those e-mails we exchanged."

Cam's face was furiously red, but he didn't seem displeased with the affectionate greeting. "Were you the one who wrote the messages? I didn't even know if you were a boy or a girl."

"I'm a girl," she said happily. "And I wrote the messages." She then began circulating among the group, shaking hands and getting their names.

"She's cute," Kesha commented. "Very, you know, healthy looking."

"They all look like that out here," Ashley informed her. "Californians are like a whole separate ethnic group. Look at Travis. He's acting like he's leading a delegation into a foreign country."

Jake had to acknowledge that Travis was in top form. This was the kind of situation he'd been brought up to deal with—meeting strangers with charm and friendly dignity. He began what sounded like a prepared speech.

"We're very pleased to be here, Charlotte, and we look forward to meeting others who survived the disaster that has fallen on Earth. As the remaining population, it is incumbent upon us to create a future for our planet."

"Pompous ass," Ashley muttered.

Jake grimaced. "He thinks he's in charge."

"We had to let him think that to make him fly us here," Ashley reminded him.

"Yeah, well, I don't want him speaking for the whole group," Jake declared, and he went up to Charlotte. "Hi, I'm Jake. What's your situation here?"

"First things first," Charlotte said. "You guys must be wiped out. Get on the bus and I'll take us back to the farm."

"The farm?" Martina repeated, but Charlotte didn't explain.

Ashley spoke to Jake excitedly. "A farm! Maybe this means real food!"

"I can't believe you're thinking about food at a time like this," Jake said. But now that she'd planted the seed in his head, he realized that he couldn't remember the last time he'd had something fresh to eat. Suddenly, all he could think about was a juicy red apple.

Travis began to direct everyone to go onto the bus. Annoyed, Jake boarded and took the seat immediately behind the bus driver's place. Ashley sat beside him. When Travis got on, he saw Jake at the head of the bus, and frowned slightly, but he didn't say anything. He and Donna took the front row seats on the other side of the aisle.

Charlotte took her place in the driver's seat and started the motor. "We're off!" she called out gaily.

Jake leaned forward. "Your streets must be like ours back in New York. We can't move more than a few feet without being blocked. How can you drive here?"

"Watch me," Charlotte said. She yanked on the gear shift and put the bus in reverse. This was no problem on the vast expanse of the landing field. She was able to maneuver around the small planes, and she picked up speed as she drove them down a runway. Once outside the airport, she pulled the bus up a hill and onto a deserted stretch of road.

"Closed for construction," she called out. "It was hit bad in the last earthquake."

"Is it safe to drive on now?" Travis asked.

Charlotte laughed. "As safe as any road in California. Watch out for cracks bigger than us."

Ashley grabbed Jake's hand, but it wasn't out of

fear. "I'm excited," she confided. "I like her— she's cool."

"Yeah, she seems to know what she's doing," Jake agreed.

"Do you think she's their leader?" Ashley wondered.

"I guess we'll find out soon enough," Jake replied.

"This could be interesting," Ashley said. "I can't picture Travis dealing with a female on an equal level."

"He won't have to," Jake said.

"What do you mean?"

"I'm not going to let him push us around," Jake told her. "He won't be making decisions for us."

"Who will?" Ashley asked. "You?"

"Us." He turned to look out the window. He could see the overpasses and cloverleafs of the elaborate and complicated freeway system for which Los Angeles was famous. They were clogged with unmoving, vacant cars and trucks, just like the streets in New York. "This road can't go on forever," he remarked to Ashley. "Where is she going to go when it ends?"

They soon found out. The bus approached the entrance that marked the end of the roadwork. Charlotte aimed the vehicle through a break in the barrier and drove onto a construction site. The bus bounced along the uneven terrain and around the skeleton of a building. On the other side, it came out into what looked like a suburban neighborhood. The street in front of them was impassable, of course. But Charlotte simply dragged the bus onto a wide front lawn. She knocked over a pink flamingo and careened across the grass.

This was how they traveled—not on roads but over front lawns, through backyards, and around swimming pools and tennis courts. At one point, they found themselves cutting across a mammoth golf course.

"Look! The Pacific Ocean!" Shalini cried out.

"Oh, man, I can see the waves!" David moaned in ecstasy. "Surf city, here I come!"

Ashley turned around in her seat and faced Martina. "We'll have to go shopping for swimsuits."

"And suntan lotion," Martina added happily.

"I'll show you my favorite stores," Charlotte promised. "Isn't shopping fun when you don't have to pay for anything?"

"Wait a second," Jake broke in. "We're not here for a vacation, you know." But he could understand how they were feeling. After the grit and grime and cement of Manhattan, California looked like paradise, especially since they were now way beyond the city of Los Angeles itself. There were trees here, the skies were a brilliant blue, and the sun was shining. It wasn't exactly the countryside—there were too many grand houses spotting the terrain. But even so, there was the sense of space, the feeling one could lie back and relax. Strange, how even an unpopulated New York City could still feel crowded and intense.

"This girl can *drive*," Ashley said with approval, and Jake agreed. She handled the bus as if it were a race car in the Indy 500, avoiding trees and mailboxes and generally managing to keep them at a steady pace. Jake guessed that all the passengers on the bus were impressed with her skill. As New Yorkers, they didn't have much driving experience. Some of them probably didn't even have licenses. Charlotte, on the other hand, had obviously grown up behind the wheel of a car. California really was an entirely different world.

The houses became farther and farther separated, and they couldn't see the ocean anymore. Clearly, they were moving inland, and they crossed a field where Jake felt sure that cows or some kind of animal had once grazed.

"We're almost there," Charlotte called out.

Moments later, they were climbing up a wide driveway, which terminated in front of a low, long, Spanish-style house, extending beyond their view on both sides.

Charlotte stopped the bus. As they all began to get off, she ran on ahead and opened a set of wide double doors that led into what had to be a living room.

It was cool and airy inside. The furniture was light-colored; there were colorful Mexican wall hangings and lots of plants.

"This is beautiful," Ashley enthused. "How did you find this place?"

"It's home," Charlotte told her. "I grew up here."

Martina was in awe. "It's huge! You must have had a big family."

Charlotte nodded. "There were twenty-three of us." She laughed at their reaction. "It was a commune," she explained. "My parents and some friends got it started back in 1969. It was just this one room back then. They've been building and adding on to it for the past thirty years.''

In Jake's mind, that explained the bus. ''Were they hippies?'' he asked.

''Yeah, I guess that's what you'd call them,'' Charlotte answered. ''They just needed to live outside the mainstream, y'know? They wanted to create their own special world, away from the cold, harsh city.''

''Isolationists,'' Travis declared. ''Did they arm themselves?''

''Oh, no, not at all,'' Charlotte demurred. ''They wanted a world where people cared about each other, an interdependent world, where everyone worked and played together. They just wanted to live with good friends, good food, good music, and to raise their kids like brothers and sisters. They decided to create a world where people are responsible for each other.''

It all sounded very California to Jake. Donna obviously didn't get it. ''You mean you lived in the same house with people you weren't related to?''

''Not by blood,'' Charlotte admitted. ''By love.''

The jaded New Yorkers were giving one another meaningful looks now. Charlotte must have seen their skepticism. ''No, really,'' she insisted. ''We were a family. Not in the conventional sense, but still a family. Just like you.''

''We're not a family,'' Alex informed her quickly. ''What makes you think we're a family?''

Jake hastened to explain. ''We were all in the same class at Madison High. When we came out of class one day, everyone else was gone.''

''Yeah, Cam wrote me about how you were

alone together in New York," Charlotte said. "But that was a couple of months ago. I figured by now you must be like a family."

David laughed. "Are you kidding? Most of us don't even like each other."

"Some of us do," Martina retorted stoutly.

"Did your whole family survive the Disappearance?" Ashley asked her, but now Charlotte had started out of the vast room and was beckoning them to follow her. She led them outside to the back where the house formed three sides around a courtyard that contained a swimming pool. Beyond that, Jake could see what looked like a large vegetable garden, a small barn, and an orchard. The orchard made him think of apples again, and his stomach rumbled.

It was a very loud rumble. He started in embarrassment when people around him turned to look.

Charlotte wasn't shocked. Instead, dismay crossed her face and she exclaimed, "Oh, how stupid of me! You guys must be starving. Come on inside. I've got dinner all ready for you." She steered them toward another door which led into a real country kitchen, in the center of which was a huge round wooden table that could seat at least a dozen. The kitchen was shiny and bright and spotlessly clean. Jake thought that this communal family had to be very well organized, if Charlotte was any example. He wondered where they were now, and how and why they'd survived.

But he stopped thinking about that when he was hit by smells he hadn't experienced in a long time.

"It's nothing fancy," Charlotte apologized. She brought over a huge kettle of steaming vegetable soup. Along with this came a big green salad spotted with bright red tomatoes and sweet onions, fresh corn on the cob, and a basket of hot, fragrant bread. The cries of delight only ceased when their mouths were too full to speak.

"This is fantastic!" Ashley exclaimed. "You know, when I was modeling, I used to have fantasies of eating all the homemade bread I could get my hands on."

"Well, eat up," Charlotte told her. "There's plenty more."

"Ohmigosh." Kesha gasped. "Is that butter? Real butter?" She slathered a chunk on her ear of corn. "Where did you get butter?"

"Obviously, this community was more farsighted than we were," Travis stated. "They froze the perishables before they could go bad."

"But this tastes so fresh," Cam remarked.

"It *is* fresh," Charlotte said. "I have a cow. I churned this butter myself."

For a moment, everyone stopped eating. "You've got a cow?" Kesha asked. "Didn't all your animals disappear? Ours did, less than a week after the people."

"Oh, sure, all the animals here disappeared, too," Charlotte assured her. "Except for this one cow. And a chicken."

"Why didn't they disappear?" Jake asked.

Charlotte looked uncomfortable. "I don't know. Why didn't *you* disappear?"

She had a point. Nobody understood why they'd been chosen. Or not chosen.

"Who wants dessert?" Charlotte asked. "I've got strawberries."

"Strawberries?" Cam repeated.

"Big, fat, sweet strawberries," Charlotte said. "And I can whip up some fresh cream to put on them."

Travis yawned, then clapped a hand to his mouth. "Excuse me!" he begged, looking stricken.

Donna provided him with an excuse for his poor behavior. "Travis did all the flying today," she reported importantly to Charlotte.

Charlotte looked suitably impressed. "And you've got jet lag too. I'll show you where you can lie down."

While most of the group followed Charlotte out of the room, Jake, Ashley, and Cam remained at the table. Ashley sank back in her seat with a sigh of satisfaction. "I haven't felt this good in ages."

"It's really nice here," Jake said. "Charlotte's great. A little strange, maybe."

"This is California," Ashley said by way of explanation.

Jake looked at Cam. "What's your problem?"

Cam was looking unusually thoughtful. "I was just thinking . . ." he said.

"About what?" Jake asked.

"Strawberries."

Jake and Ashley exchanged looks. Nobody could ever really understand the way Cam's mind worked.

Charlotte returned to the kitchen. "Aren't you guys tired?"

"I'm getting a second wind," Cam said. "I'd like to see more of the farm."

Jake and Ashley decided to go along with them. The sun was going down, but there was still enough light to see where they were going as Charlotte led them around to the side of the house they hadn't seen yet. No one had really looked out the windows.

Ashley stood very still, looking out at the expanse of land that stood before them. "What's that?"

Charlotte was silent for a moment. Then she answered. "It's a labyrinth."

That wasn't enough for Ashley. "What's a labyrinth?"

Jake was curious, too. He'd never seen anything like what he was looking at now.

It was an area that he estimated to be the size of a school gymnasium. There were some trees, some flower beds, but that wasn't what they were staring at. On the grass was a path, lined with small stones.

It wasn't a normal path—at least, it wasn't a path like Jake had ever seen before. It didn't appear to lead in a direct line across the expanse of grass. It crossed the lawn in a circular, twisting pattern.

It wasn't a maze. Jake had been in a maze once before, and he hadn't enjoyed it. A maze was a puzzle. It ran between shrubbery or walls, there were twists and turns that you had to choose, and it was very easy to get lost. True, he'd only been six years old when he'd encountered the maze at the home of some friends of his grandparents in Florida. But he hadn't forgotten the general sense of disorientation.

This thing—this labyrinth, as Charlotte called it—didn't make him uncomfortable. For one thing, there was no shrubbery along the sides of the path, no walls. It didn't look like anyone had to make a choice about which path to take—there was only one path. But what was the point? If you couldn't get lost or confused, if the object wasn't to find your way to the other end . . . what was the meaning of the labyrinth?

He was trying to think of an appropriate way to ask this, when Cam got right to the point. "What's it for?" he asked.

Charlotte spoke carefully. "It helps you think."

"Think about what?" Ashley asked.

"Whatever you want to think about." She must have realized that wasn't enough of an answer, because she sighed and tried to explain.

"My parents and their friends, they created this long ago, when they first moved here, before I was born. It's important to our family. As you follow the path of the labyrinth, your mind becomes very quiet. And you see more . . . about yourself. And everyone else. And what you mean and what you are."

Jake had heard of the New-Age-cult-mystical-herbal ways of this part of the country. "Very California," he whispered to Ashley.

Charlotte heard him. "No," she said, "it's nothing new. There have been labyrinths since at least two thousand years before the birth of Christ. At least, that's what my parents told me." After a moment, she added, "And I believe them."

Jake didn't know what to say.

Charlotte continued. "You walk into the labyrinth," she said, "and you begin to understand."

"Understand what?" Jake asked.

Charlotte's voice became dreamy. "How to focus. How to find peace and enlightenment. How to heal ourselves.''

"Heal ourselves from what?" Ashley wanted to know.

"From what we've become," Charlotte replied. "You walk, you follow, you go to the center, and then . . ."

"And then what?" Cam asked. His voice was hoarse.

"You know," Charlotte said simply. "You just . . . know."

Know what? Jake wanted to ask. But even in the dim, fading light, he could see Charlotte's face. She looked . . . frightened.

"Are you okay?" he asked.

"Of course," she replied.

"Let's go walk the path," Ashley said.

"No!" Charlotte cried out. And then she said, "I mean, not now. It's getting too dark." She pointed. "In the center . . . that's where I was when it happened. The Disappearance. I was in the center."

"Where were the others?" Jake asked.

She didn't answer.

Cam spoke. "Charlotte? Where are the others?"

After another few seconds, Charlotte spoke.

"There are no others."

three

"that is one weird chick."

That was David's comment the next morning when Jake reported what he and Ashley and Cam had learned the night before.

"That was all she said?" Travis asked. " 'There are no others'? She didn't say what happened to them?"

Jake shrugged. "I assume they all just disappeared when everyone else on Earth did."

"Then why is *she* still here?" Donna asked.

"Why are the rest of us still here?" Kesha countered. "She probably doesn't know any more than we do. Possibly less." She turned to Jake. "Did you ask her what she knows?"

Jake shook his head. "We were all pretty shook up."

"And exhausted," Ashley added. "She didn't feel like answering questions, and we didn't feel like asking them. She said she'd explain everything in the morning."

"Well, it's morning now," Travis declared, "and I, for one, want some answers."

He joined David at the window. "What is she doing, anyway?"

"Walking the labyrinth," Cam said. "She told us a little about it last night."

"Very weird," David said again. "It looks like she's talking to herself."

"That's called meditation," Ashley informed him.

"Talking to herself," Alex repeated. "Isn't that the first sign of insanity?" Shalini edged closer to him, and he put a protective arm around her.

Martina was horrified. "I still can't believe it. The poor girl! She's been on her own here for two months!"

Alex wasn't quite so sympathetic. "The bitch! She lured us out here, telling us she had a whole community here."

Donna wasn't pleased with the situation, either. "This could be a trap," she said nervously. "Maybe she's not even human. She could be one of them, and she got us out here so they can—so they can—"

"Can do what?" Ashley asked. "Donna, if they wanted to zap us off the face of the Earth, they could have done it back in New York."

"Travis, what do you think?" Donna asked plaintively.

"I think we should get out of here," he said. "If we're not trapped."

"We're not trapped," Cam said calmly. "We can leave anytime we want." He gazed out the window where Charlotte was walking along the twisted path. "Personally, I think we should stick around."

They all gathered at the window and watched as Charlotte moved along the labyrinth. The dirt path twisted and turned, but it seemed to lead directly to one place, the center of the circle. Charlotte reached the center and stood there, very still.

"How did she survive out here in the middle of nowhere?" Martina wondered.

"It couldn't have been that hard for her," Cam said. "This farm provides food. And she could drive anywhere to get other stuff."

"I mean *emotionally*," Martina said. "How did she manage to keep from going crazy with no one to talk to?"

"She's strong," Kesha said. "She's tough. She's made it on her own; she hasn't needed anyone. I admire that."

"Oh, Kesha." Donna groaned. "Everybody needs people."

Kesha didn't bother to contradict her. She and Donna had this argument about once a month. Donna firmly believed that a social life was as necessary to a human being as food and water. Kesha felt they'd all function better if they could learn to be more independent, less needy. Like Charlotte.

"Let's go back to New York," Alex said. "At least we know there are fifteen other human beings there. If we're going to get any kind of army pulled together—"

"An army!" Jake interrupted. "Alex, get real! Whatever's out there has the power to make the entire population of Earth disappear! What kind of army can fight that?"

"We could try," Alex said stubbornly. "I'm not giving up without a fight."

Kesha was about to explode. "Try what?" she

cried. "Give up what? And who are you going to fight? That girl?"

Shalini actually voiced an opinion. "And I don't think we should go back to New York and leave her behind."

Alex spoke to her sharply. "She's not like us, Shalini."

"Alex is right," Cam said unexpectedly. "She's not like us. She's better than us. She knows something we don't know. So why don't we just talk to her and find out what that is?"

"She's coming back now," Kesha reported from the window.

They all stared as Charlotte walked into the room. Charlotte tried to stare back, but her eyes were darting around. She had to know she was on the defensive.

Alex stepped forward in an aggressive manner. "Okay, we want to know what's going on."

"Wait a minute," Travis interjected. "You're not in charge here." He approached Charlotte. "Um . . . we want to know what's going on. Now. Why did you lie and tell us you had a community of people here?"

Jake spoke more kindly, but he, too, was firm. "You said you'd answer questions in the morning, Charlotte."

She nodded, but she hesitated. "I'm not sure you're going to understand. You haven't walked the path."

Kesha was skeptical. "Is this one of those California things? Walk around in circles and the truth will be revealed?"

"Not exactly," Charlotte admitted. "But you'll

know more than you do now. Well, some of you will.''

It was clear to Alex that he wouldn't be one of them. ''What's that supposed to mean?''

''You have to want to believe. You have to open your mind.''

David groaned. ''This is sounding just a little too *X-Files* for me.''

''California,'' Kesha murmured again.

Charlotte's eyes flashed. ''Hey, knock it off! Stop dumping on California! Okay, some strange ideas have come from here, but maybe that's because we're a little more open-minded than you guys. We're not sophisticated, jaded, know-it-all New Yorkers. . . . Personally, I prefer to think there are things in the world I *don't* know. I'd like to think there's something left to *learn*.'' Her voice rose with each word, and ''learn'' was practically shrieked. Travis took a step back, and the others all looked faintly alarmed. Kesha wondered if maybe the girl wasn't just a little off balance.

Cam was nodding. ''Yeah, I'm with you,'' he said to Charlotte. ''I mean, California has produced its share of nutcases, but at least you're not afraid to think that maybe things aren't exactly as they seem.''

His words had a calming effect on Charlotte. She took a deep breath. ''Thank you.'' She and Cam actually gave each other little smiles of complicity.

They looked like they were sharing a secret, and Kesha wanted in on it. ''Are you going to tell us what this is all about now?''

Charlotte sighed. ''I'm not sure where to start.''

"Start off by telling us why you lied," Alex demanded.

"Isn't that obvious?" Cam asked.

"Maybe to you, brainiac," David said. "The rest of us aren't so quick on the uptake."

"Speak for yourself," Jake said. He turned to Charlotte. "I'll bet you were afraid we wouldn't come if we thought there was only one person out here."

Charlotte nodded. "Exactly."

"Why was it so important to get us here?" Kesha asked.

Donna proposed an answer. "Because she was lonely, Kesha! Can you blame her?"

Charlotte didn't say anything. Cam looked at her quizzically. "Is that really why you wanted us here?" he asked.

"Not exactly," she admitted. "Yeah, I was kind of lonely at first. It got better . . ." her voice trailed off, as if she were afraid to say more.

Kesha went back to the window. "When did that thing appear?"

Shalini ventured a guess. "Was it made by some kind of alien spaceship?"

Charlotte actually laughed, a nice, big, normal sort of laugh. "Are you kidding? My *father* made that labyrinth. And I can assure you, he's no alien." She turned toward the window and looked out at the circle. "Actually, they all created it together, the original members of the commune. And it's not some spooky, new California thing. Labyrinths have been used as a form of meditation tool for hundreds of years. The commune members thought it would be a way of helping them all to get along with each other.''

''I read a book about meditation,'' Martina said, ''but it said you had to sit very still in one place.''

''That's one way,'' Charlotte said. ''This is another. The labyrinth is supposed to be a metaphor for life. See, there are lots of twists and turns, but no matter how you walk it, ultimately you get to the center. So the path may be different for each one of us, but we all have to start in the same place, and we all end up in the same place.''

Donna looked blank. ''Huh?''

''We're all born; we all die,'' Kesha explained.

Now Donna was alarmed. ''You mean, the center of the labyrinth is death?''

''It's a goal,'' Charlotte told her. ''When you get to the center, you've reached the goal.''

''*What* goal?'' David asked.

Charlotte didn't answer.

''Did you use the labyrinth a lot?'' Cam asked her. ''Before?''

''Once in a while,'' Charlotte said. ''Whenever I felt anxious or angry or I wasn't getting along with people, I walked the path. I walked to the center, I cleared my head, I was able to see things differently. That's what each of us did, whenever we felt like something was wrong.''

''And when you came out the problem was solved?'' Jake asked.

''No. But you understood the problem better. And you could start dealing with it. That's what the walk gives you. Wisdom.''

Kesha faced the girl. ''Are you saying that you

understand why everyone else in the world has disappeared?''

"Maybe.''

"But you can't explain it to us because we wouldn't understand.''

"Yes.''

"Do you know why they didn't take us?''

Charlotte shook her head. "No. And I don't think it's right to say 'they.' ''

"It, then. He, she—whatever. Do you know why it didn't take you?''

This time, Charlotte nodded. "It didn't have to take me. It joined me.''

There was a silence as each member of the group absorbed these words and tried to make sense out of them.

David made a choking sound. "Geez, this sounds like something out of *Invasion of the Body Snatchers*. You go in this labyrinth thing, something gets inside you, and then you know things you didn't know before? If you don't mind, I think I'll stay out of there.''

Alex looked triumphant. "See, I was right—she's with them! I say we use her as a bargaining chip. We don't let her back into the labyrinth till the rest of the people are free.''

"No, no!'' Charlotte cried in frustration. "You don't understand! The labyrinth isn't some sort of secret path to another world. It just brings us to a peaceful place, so we can make connections and find the part of ourselves that we lost.''

"That's the goal, isn't it?'' Cam asked suddenly. "To reconcile. To become complete.''

Charlotte beamed at him. "Exactly! That's always been the goal. That's why I was able to make the connection. The labyrinth isn't magic; it doesn't guarantee a connection. And I guess the connection could be made outside the labyrinth. But the labyrinth makes it easier to get there.''

''Get where?'' David asked plaintively. ''Connect to what?''

Donna appeared to be confused, too. ''Travis, what are we going to do?''

''I want to speak to whoever is in charge,'' Travis stated. ''The leader of this—whatever it is.''

''Oh, Travis, don't be ridiculous.'' Kesha snorted.

''No, wait a minute,'' Jake said. ''Travis has a point.''

Kesha couldn't believe Jake had just said that. And no one looked more surprised than Travis. ''I do?''

''We have to connect,'' Jake said. ''We need to communicate with it—or them or whatever.'' He looked out the window. ''I want to go into the labyrinth.''

Ashley let out an involuntary gasp.

Shalini spoke timidly. ''Couldn't we just invite them to come here?''

''They tried that,'' Kesha said suddenly, ''back in New York. Remember Jonah? Rosa recognized him. She said he was one of them.''

''Why didn't he tell us anything?'' Donna wanted to know.

''Maybe he didn't know how,'' Kesha said. ''Like Martina said she didn't know how she reached Rosa. We could be just as hard for them to understand as they are to us!''

"He took Adam," Jake said. "Remember Adam? No one knew him very well."

"Maybe that's why he went with Jonah," Cam said. "Maybe he wanted to go." He looked at Charlotte.

Charlotte smiled. "Yes," she said. "You can't be forced. You have to want this."

Kesha spoke up. "I agree with Jake. Someone's got to go into that labyrinth and make contact."

"Exactly," Jake said.

"Only I don't see why it should be you, Jake." She turned to Charlotte. "Couldn't we all go in?"

"I don't know," Charlotte said. "I went in by myself. If too many people go in at the same time, it might be hard to really concentrate."

"You're not getting me in there," David declared.

Travis spoke unexpectedly. "I want to go first."

"Why?" Jake asked.

"You asked me to join you and lead you to where we had to go. I got you here, but it looks like this isn't the ultimate destination. I'll go first."

"Now, wait a minute, Travis," Jake began, but Charlotte stopped him.

"You don't have to decide right this minute. And you should eat first. I've found that the labyrinth is easier to walk when you're not hungry."

Everyone began to move toward the kitchen. Kesha hung back and motioned to Jake. Ashley remained behind, too.

"Travis can't handle this," Kesha said in a low voice. "Not alone."

"I was thinking the same thing," Jake admitted. "I want to go into the labyrinth with him."

"You think he'll agree to that?"

"Maybe. If I approach him the right way . . ."

"I could go," Kesha said, but Jake shook his head.

"You and Travis are going to work together? I don't think so, Kesha."

Kesha had to admit that they wouldn't make an ideal couple.

"I want to go, too," Ashley declared.

"No."

Ashley's eyes flashed. Oh no, Kesha thought, here we go again. Another lover's spat.

"I have to go," Ashley said. "I'm supposed to find Corey, to save him. That's why he's been appearing to me."

"I'll find him," Jake said. "Please, Ashley, don't try to come. Look, I know this sounds like sexist garbage, but if you're there, all I'll be able to think about is you. And I have to keep my attention focused on Travis. He can't be trusted to handle this on his own."

"Jake's got a point," Kesha said to Ashley.

Ashley looked at her in annoyance. "I can't believe you're taking his side! Where's your loyalty?"

Kesha backed away. "You two can fight about this. I'm out of here." She left the room. But she lingered just outside the entrance. She wanted to hear what they decided.

"Think about it," Jake was saying urgently. "It's going to be hard enough convincing Travis to let me come with him. If you try to come too . . . oh, Ashley, it's just going to get more and more complicated. And Travis can't deal with a girl as an equal partner, a member of his team. You know that.''

''Yes, I do know that,'' Ashley said. ''But that doesn't mean we should give in to his chauvinistic attitude.''

''But this isn't the time or the place to start re-educating him,'' Jake said gently. ''Ashley, the whole world is at stake. Let's see if we can get things back to normal. And then, I promise you, we'll work to make things better.''

There was a moment of silence. ''Promise?'' Ashley said finally.

''Promise,'' Jake replied. ''But there's something I want you to promise me, too.''

''What?''

''That no matter what happens, you won't follow me in there. Even if everyone else goes running into that labyrinth, you'll stay here.''

''Why?''

Now Kesha had to strain to hear what he was saying. His voice was low and husky.

''You remember what we figured out in Central Park? When my mind started to leave my body and you brought it back? We knew that whatever was going on, whatever had happened in the world, it had something to do with love. Remember?''

''Yes.''

''I need to know . . . that someone here on Earth loves me enough to bring me back.''

''All right,'' Ashley said. ''I'll stay.''

''No matter what?''

''No matter what.''

''Promise?''

''I promise.''

Then there was nothing more to hear, but Kesha knew what was happening. They were kissing, they were holding each other tightly, they were caught up in some kind of understanding, some kind of communication that Kesha couldn't understand.

It hurt her to think that she might never understand.

four

Jake had expected Travis to make a real stink about this, but for once he'd overestimated his classmate's ego. Travis actually seemed relieved at the prospect of having a companion on his journey.

He made perfunctory objections, of course. "It isn't necessary, Jake. You'll be putting yourself in danger. I'm certainly capable of handling this on my own." But after a moment, he added, "I suppose it wouldn't hurt to have an aide."

"Exactly," Jake began, but Travis held up his hand. He hadn't finished.

"Of course, you'll have to understand that I'm in charge of this mission."

This was clearly not the time for Jake to assert himself. He smiled thinly. "I'll be glad to assist you, Travis."

Charlotte approached them. "Would you like me to show you how to walk the path?"

Jake looked toward the field where the labyrinth was laid out. "Is there a special way to approach it? Some trick we need to be aware of?"

Charlotte shook her head. "You can't get lost. It's not like a maze—there are no wrong turns. No dead ends. You go at your own pace, and you can pause whenever you like. You can—"

Travis stopped her. "We don't need for you to teach us how to walk, Charlotte. I've been doing it since I was one."

"But there are ways to think," Charlotte insisted, "a way to *be*, while you're walking. You can't just skip along the path to the center, and expect something to happen when you get there. You have to clear your head, free your mind. Do you understand?"

Travis's expression made it clear that he didn't.

Jake hated putting himself on the same level as Travis, but there was no avoiding it this time. He had no more understanding of this labyrinth than Travis did.

Charlotte sighed. "Just be receptive, okay? Let it happen."

The entire group walked with Travis and Jake to the edge of the labyrinth. Nobody seemed to know what to say. Donna was crying, of course. Jake thought she was behaving like a woman who was sending her husband off to war. Travis stepped onto the path, then looked back.

No one knew what to say. "Bon voyage" seemed somehow inadequate.

Jake turned to Ashley. "Remember, you promised me. No matter what, you'll stay here."

"I promise," she said. As if to demonstrate this, she stepped back from the entrance to the labyrinth and went to a small bench a few yards away, where she sat down to watch.

Travis had already begun walking the path. He was moving too fast, Jake thought. Jake didn't know anything about clearing or freeing the mind, but he suspected that it wasn't an activity that should be conducted at such a rapid pace.

But that was about all he knew as he set off on the path. How could a person empty his mind and not think of anything? At the moment, all he could think about was Ashley. Was she keeping her promise, was she still sitting on that bench? He wanted to turn around, to look back at her, but he knew that wasn't the right thing to do.

If he couldn't clear his mind, would it help to concentrate on something? An image, perhaps, like a flower? The sun, the moon, the stars, Ashley's face . . . no. A word, then—but what word? Or a sound, a musical note, a song? No . . . he should concentrate on a feeling. Fear? That couldn't be right. Anticipation . . . no, *hope*. Yes, that was the emotion to fixate on, hope. Not any specific hope, like wealth or a cure for cancer or even success of this crazy mission . . . just hope.

And as he began to hope, he became aware of another sensation—a lightness in his step. It was as if the cares and concerns he'd brought into the labyrinth were leaving him, dropping away from his body and making him almost weightless. He could feel his tension begin to fade, leaving him calm and relaxed. His walk became rhythmic, and he had the sensation of being secure and balanced. He felt like he could walk a tightrope with no problem. He could see Travis ahead of him, but only as a dim, vague sort of realization of another presence in the labyrinth. It had no impact on his sense of harmony and well-being. Then he realized he was there, in the center, and it was as if he'd floated the last few paces. Travis was there, too.

He didn't want to speak to Travis. He *couldn't* speak to Travis. He couldn't greet him, or shake his hand, or acknowledge him in any way. He couldn't even see him.

Curiously, he realized he wasn't scared. He couldn't see, hear, smell, touch, but he felt no apprehension at all. Was this what it was like to be dead? No, he couldn't be dead, because he was totally conscious, completely awake and aware. But it was a funny sort of awareness, with no sensations. He was floating. . . .

He recalled what Martina had said—that the experience was like getting nitrous oxide, laughing gas, in the dentist's office. Jake had never asked his dentist for laughing gas. Next time he had an appointment, he would. He didn't think he'd mind the sound of the drill if he was in this condition.

He wasn't alone. He knew this the same way he knew he wasn't dead. He just knew. He was being contacted, and he knew who was contacting him.

Jonah.

Yes.

How amazing. No words were said, nothing was heard, but there had been a communication.

What's going on here? Who's there?

That was Travis.

Travis, it's me, Jake. I'm here. Jonah is here, too.

Who's in charge here? I want to speak to the person in charge.

Jake didn't know how he recognized Travis's words when he couldn't hear, when the actual physical sense of hearing didn't exist. But the con-

nection was there, the meaning was understood.
What was more, he could actually comprehend the
urgency in Travis's voice. He tried to lighten the
mood.

*Hey, Travis, where are your manners? You re-
member Jonah from New York, the guy you kicked
out of the Community. Maybe now would be a good
time to apologize.*

*Are you crazy? I don't owe him an apology!
He's one of them—he kidnapped the people of our
planet!*

Hey, ease up, man! But Jake realized there was
no way Travis could have known he was kidding.
He'd have to watch everything he ''said''—or
thought or however he was communicating. Without any physical ability to modify a comment, all
words would be taken at face value.

Jonah replied to Travis's earlier question.

There is no person in charge. We are one.

Was Jonah mocking them? Jake wondered. Was
he laughing at their predicament? Did he feel sorry
for them, did he care about what had happened? It
was impossible to tell from his words.

Who makes the rules? Jake asked. *Who makes
the decisions?* Then he added, *I'm not arguing, I'm
just curious.* He wished he could show Jonah that
he wasn't challenging him or anything like that. If
he could make a friendly gesture, shake Jonah's
hand, slap his back . . . if he could just *smile,* he'd
feel better about what he was saying, would know
it wouldn't be misinterpreted.

We rule. We decide.

Jake, what the hell is going on here?

Now Jake wondered if there was something

other than urgency in Travis's tone. Was Travis beginning to panic? Or was Jake interpreting the mood correctly? Travis wasn't prone to panic. He was the kind of person who always managed to look like he was in control, even when he wasn't. He was big on maintaining dignity and an air of authority. Even when he didn't know what he was doing, he could act like he did.

But Travis couldn't act *here*, wherever they were. Travis had no face, no body, no commanding voice with which he could convey an image, become a presence. He could only *be*. He had no means to intimidate or bully or seduce.

And even though he had no voice, Jake could detect a shrillness.

I want—I demand— Let me see someone now.

Travis, haven't you figured it out yet? You can't see; you can't do anything.

Could a sound that was only perceptible as thought be characterized as a shriek, a scream? Jake gave up on Travis and concentrated on Jonah.

Jonah, what are you?

We are.

Can you tell— Can you communicate to me more about what you are? Like, in comparison to what I am?

We exist. We survive. We are many; we are one. We were once as you are. Separate and unique. Now we are together.

Why? What happened to change you?

Jonah told them.

We did not obey the laws of nature. We fought our own world, battling it in order to force the environment to perform more efficiently, to satisfy our physical desires more quickly, more completely. More in keeping with what we perceived to be our needs. We demanded perfection in our nourishment, so we did not allow our food to develop as it would naturally. We demanded total comfort, and we treated our atmosphere so that we would never be too cold, too hot, too wet, too dry. We experimented with life, allowing only the most perfect beings to be born. We wasted; we polluted. We tormented the environment, and in the end the environment we created betrayed us. We could not retain our physical selves. And with the loss of our bodies came the loss of feeling.

Jake spoke. *But how could you survive without any bodies?*

We were forced to adapt. We came together, to become a force that could survive. Our energy came together. While the body disintegrated, the mind grew stronger. And so, we exist.

Jake tried to comprehend this.

But what do you do?

There was no response.

Jonah, you were on Earth—you saw what we do. Do you eat? Do you—do you laugh, do you cry, do you sleep, do you make love?

Another silence, and then a response: *We survive. We exist. That's all we can do.*

It sounded like an episode Jake had once seen on the old *Twilight Zone* television series. These—these entities, this species, they could not "do" at all; they could only "be." He wouldn't have believed a word of this if he weren't experiencing it himself. It dawned on him that he wasn't hungry or thirsty, and that although he could remember the acts of eating and drinking he couldn't recall what it felt like to have those needs.

Was Travis having the same revelations? Jake addressed him.

Travis, do you hear what he is saying? Do you comprehend this?

There was no answer, but there was some kind of response. At first, Jake couldn't identify what he was understanding. Travis was in the process of something. Jake finally gave it a name. Travis was falling apart. He couldn't handle this—he couldn't absorb it. Was it the information or the manner in which it was being conveyed that had sent Travis over the edge? What would happen to him?

He will survive.

It was Jonah who was telling him this. But Jake wasn't aware of having asked the question.

You can read my mind?

Our level of connection is more developed than yours. We have had to compensate for the lack of physical sensation. Our minds are strong.

Jake considered this. The possibilities were obvious.

Strong enough to remove the entire population from the face of the Earth?

Yes.

He knew this would be an appropriate moment to feel anger. Certainly, he knew anger. He remembered anger. He thought he could feel it now, if he tried, if he concentrated.

But that's wrong! It's legally and ethically wrong! Just because we had bodies and you didn't, you had no right to take ours. A poor person doesn't have the right to steal from a rich person. Don't you have any morals?

Your laws are not our laws. Your morals are not our morals.

Do you have any morals at all?

We take care of one another. This is our moral obligation. This is our priority. We cannot extend this obligation to the universe. Your people cannot even extend it to one another.

Now, what the hell was *that* supposed to mean?

We exist, we survive.

He was hearing this now, again and again, in a silent chorus. He realized the statement wasn't coming from Jonah or from Jonah's kind. Human minds were communicating this to him.

Ashley hadn't left her position on the bench just outside the labyrinth. The figures of Jake and Travis were still visible. She wasn't sure what she should expect to see next. Would they slowly dissolve, fade away, like she'd seen the people on Earth do in the security videos they'd found in various stores? Would they look like they were beamed off the planet, like the crew of the starship *Enterprise* on *Star Trek*?

Donna sat beside her. It had been almost an hour since the boys had reached the center. Everyone else had given up the watch.

"I think I saw Travis move," Donna said.

Ashley thought it was her imagination. But she put a hand over her eyes to shut out the sun's glare and squinted in an effort to see details. Then she hopped off the bench.

"You're right."

Donna started toward the labyrinth, but Ashley grabbed her arm. "Donna, you can't go in there. Wait—they're coming out."

The two figures were coming closer. They weren't walking the path to get out of the labyrinth. They cut across the field in a direct line toward the girls.

"I guess it didn't work," Donna said.

Ashley didn't know whether to be sorry or relieved. She waved. Neither of the boys waved back. As the boys approached, she noticed there was something different about Jake. It was the way he was walking—stiffly, as if he'd been still for a very long time. Or as if he'd never walked before.

"That's not Jake," she said suddenly.

"What are you talking about?" Donna asked.

"That person who looks like Jake . . . it's not really him. And I'm sure that the person who looks like Travis isn't Travis." She could make out their faces now, and she knew she was right.

Donna clearly wasn't so sure. As soon as the two boys stepped over the boundary of the labyrinth, she ran toward Travis. The boy didn't step back or look alarmed, which should have warned Donna, Ashley thought. The real Travis hated public displays of affection.

The reality hit Donna before she could fling her arms around the person. "Travis?" she said uncertainly.

Ashley stood by her side. "It's like in Central Park, Donna. Remember?"

Donna went pale. "He took Travis's body!" she whispered.

Ashley addressed the boys. "Do you know where you are?"

"Yes," one of the boys said.

"Travis and Jake—they're with your—your people? In your world?"

"Yes," the other boy said.

"And this is just a temporary exchange, right? So you can experience this world?"

They replied together. "Yes."

She noticed how their eyes were darting about, as if they were trying to see everything at once. "Come with us," she said.

Donna looked like she was still in a state of shock, but she walked with them toward the house.

"Do you know about us?" Ashley asked.

"We know everything," the Jake look-alike said. "We have watched you. We have spoken with your kind, who visit our world."

Ashley gasped. "Then—they're all alive. Our people."

"They survive," the Travis replica told her. "They exist."

"Do you know whose body you're in?" Donna asked him.

He considered this. "It is a male body." He looked at Donna. "You have a female body."

Donna seemed to have recovered from her shock. "Yeah, well, don't let that give you any ideas."

five

kesha knew she shouldn't be astounded by what she was hearing. All the clues, the hints, the evidence—it had been there all along, ever since the Disappearance. Some sort of intelligence had to have been at work. And yet, when representatives appeared, their intelligence had been questionable. There had been the stranger Jonah, who came and left so mysteriously and never did or said anything particularly interesting, she thought. There were the childlike personas who had inhabited the bodies of Alex, Shalini, and David back in Central Park.

Now these two—whatever they were—sat at the kitchen table and made it very clear that there was an existence beyond her comprehension, and, remarkably, it was all beginning to make sense. Rosa's report of her life in this other world, Martina's experience when she changed places with her twin sister—these were all clues that indicated the existence of a life-form unlike their own. A life-form without—form.

From what she'd gathered so far, they simply existed. They couldn't experience the five senses—smell, taste, touch, sight, sound—which perhaps explained why the one in Travis's body was currently devouring a slice of cake with such intensity. They had some sort of consciousness, though, with the knowledge of everything but no physical experience. And at the same time, they seemed to have some sort of dim, collective memory of having once been physical, substantial, real. But even with this ancient history in their consciousness, they were not comfortable in these human forms. Perhaps their original forms were different. Or maybe it had been too long since they'd had any form at all.

The un-Travis had consumed his cake. He reached across the table and took David's slice from his plate.

"Whoa, buddy. If you want more, ask for it!" David said. "Don't take other people's food."

"They're not accustomed to sensations like hunger," Charlotte explained. "They can't control themselves."

David eyed the alien uneasily. "He's not going to wet his pants, is he?"

The un-Travis replied, his voice sounding eerily like—but not like—Travis's. "We have knowledge of the human need to relieve one's self of waste material. When the need becomes apparent, we will go to the appropriate place."

Cam was studying the two strangers with interest. "You say 'we,' not 'I.' Is everything in your world expressed collectively?"

"We are as one," the un-Travis said.

"But you do feel the same things at the same time?"

"I thought they couldn't feel anything," Martina said.

"It looks like they can now, in these bodies," Cam noted. "See? Right now the Jake alien is drinking a glass of water. That means he is experiencing thirst. But the Travis alien isn't thirsty, are you?"

"We are still as one," he repeated.

Cam nodded. "I think I get it. You make decisions as one. You have complete cooperation. Each mind is unique, separate, but you're bound by the same knowledge and total trust in each other, so there's never any disagreement."

Charlotte was in awe. "Cam, you're brilliant. I didn't understand any of it until I felt the spirit within me."

"Never any disagreements," Ashley echoed. "That means there would never be any reason for war."

"We have no war," the un-Jake acknowledged.

Kesha had a thought. "And if you don't need food to exist, then you don't have starvation or famine in your world. Am I right?"

Both aliens nodded.

"No hunger, no war." Kesha sighed. "Think of that."

"But no love, either," Ashley reminded her.

"No sex," David added. "You guys don't have bodies, right? So you're not divided into males and females."

"Correct," the un-Travis said.

"So . . . how do you folks, y'know—how do you *do* it?"

"I believe David is inquiring as to how you

propagate your species,'' Cam translated.

''We do not expire,'' the un-Jake said. ''Pure mental energy cannot break down.''

''They don't die,'' Donna said in amazement. ''They live forever.''

''Without love,'' Ashley said again. ''And I'm not talking about sex, David, I'm talking about love. Family love. The love of friends for each other. And romantic love too, of course. Sorry, but even with no war and no death, I don't find their so-called life very appealing.''

Because romantic love is an important part of your life, Kesha said silently. Aloud, she said, ''Their life must be so much simpler.'' Impulsively, she leaned toward them and spoke urgently. ''You have the sensation of sight now. How do we appear to you?''

They perused the group at the table, and the un-Jake spoke. ''Your skin is darker than the others','' he said to Kesha. ''You are the same color as the body which my companion inhabits.'' He looked at David. ''Your eyes have a different shape than the eyes of the others.''

''I'm black,'' Kesha informed them. ''David is Chinese. The rest are basically Caucasian. Except for Ashley, who's a little bit of everything.''

The un-Jake didn't seem terribly interested. ''Is this a significant aspect of your character?''

''Not of our character,'' Kesha said carefully.

''Race has no meaning for us,'' the un-Travis said. ''All are the same.''

''No racism,'' Kesha murmured. ''No sexism.'' It was mind-boggling. ''What else do you see when you look at us?''

The un-Travis looked at Ashley's fuzzy bits of hair. "Her hair is light-colored." His eyes moved to Donna. "Your hair is dark-colored."

"Which one looks better to you?" Kesha asked.

For once, the un-Travis seemed puzzled. "Better? On what scale? Size? Physical strength?"

"Prettier," Kesha said. "Who looks prettier to you?"

"We cannot make judgments like that," the un-Travis declared. "We understand that your species has established artificial standards that determine which physical features are pleasing to the eye."

"Beauty," Kesha said.

"We have no comprehension of this."

Kesha absorbed this information. It was dizzying.

"Would you like more cake?" Charlotte asked.

Alex had been standing just outside the kitchen entrance for about ten minutes now. "This is disgusting," he said to Shalini.

"Why do you say that?"

"Well, look at them! They're having a stinking tea party with the enemy, for crying out loud! And check out that Charlotte. She's treating the two spooks like they're honored guests. I guess that makes sense—she's half spook herself."

Alex couldn't believe what he heard next. Kesha was asking the body snatchers if it was possible to make a visit to their world, to experience it, temporarily of course. And naturally, the spooks were agreeing, so more spooks could have their bodies for a while and see how it felt.

"Are they nuts?" he asked Shalini incredulously. "Do they really think they're going to get their bodies back?"

"You got yours back before," Shalini pointed out. "And I got mine."

"Yeah, well, we were lucky."

"I don't think it's luck," Shalini said. "I don't think they can function in our bodies. Not for long. They don't know how to be human."

Alex rolled his eyes. Since when had she become such an expert on aliens?

"I want to go," Shalini said.

"What?"

"I want to visit where they come from. This is a great opportunity, Alex. I want to experience their world."

"Forget it," Alex stated. "No way."

She gazed at him mildly. "I'm going, Alex."

He'd seen that look on her face once before. It was the time when they'd seen the outline of the spaceship on the Great Lawn in Central Park, and she insisted that they bring the news back to the others. Shalini didn't assert herself very often. But when she did . . .

He wouldn't be able to stop her, but he could prevent her from going alone. Maybe it wasn't such a bad idea, anyway. How could he fight them without confronting them? If he could penetrate their world, he'd have a chance to discover their weaknesses. And if he could act on those weaknesses, he could—he could destroy them. Rescue the human population. Be a hero. Show them all what Alex Popov was really made of.

Before he could stop himself, he was in the kitchen with Shalini, announcing their intentions.

The next thing he knew, they were walking the path of the labyrinth with Donna, Kesha, Martina, and David. Then they were all in the center of the labyrinth.

And then they were—nothing. That was the only way Alex would ever be able to describe it. He had no arms, no legs, no head or body. He had no sensations of standing, walking, moving, breathing . . . and yet he was completely aware.

Alex?

Yes, I'm here.

How do you feel?

Like a ghost or something. How do you feel?

I feel free. Do you remember this? From before?

No.

Neither do I. I don't think they wanted us to remember.

Alex had to believe that was what had happened, that their memories had been taken away. Because he would never have forgotten a sensation like this.

He was aware of the existence of others around him.

Travis? Travis? That was Donna "speaking," or whatever it was they were doing to communicate.

Travis?

The response to this was faint. *Donna? Are you here?*

We're all here. Except for Ashley and Cam and Charlotte. They stayed on Earth. Wow, Travis, I can't believe how this feels—it's neat! This must be what it's like to sky dive, you know, with a parachute. You just drift along. . . . Travis? Are you still here?

Yes . . .

What's happening? Did you talk to the leader? Are you having negotiations or something? Will they let everyone go? Travis? Why won't you answer me?

I can't. I can't do anything.

None of us can do anything, Travis—that's how it is here. But we've got our brains, Travis! Travis?

I can't—this isn't me.

The pompous jerk was a disaster, Alex realized. Without his classy exterior, his uptown manners, his J. Crew clothes and his fifty-dollar haircut, he was nothing. Alex thought he'd get some pleasure from this, but it didn't happen.

He hadn't lost all feeling, though. He was very much aware of frustration and anger and something far worse. He was helpless. It was overwhelming, this simple knowledge that he was unable to form a fist or kick or shove—or do anything to defend himself.

Then, like a voice in a dream, he heard someone speaking.

You have no power here.

Who said that?

I'm Adam. From geometry class.

Adam . . . yes, the name rang a bell. Adam something—he couldn't remember his last name. But he did remember that Adam had been with them, back in the Community. He'd been one of Travis's goons . . . but he'd switched teams to join the rebels. He'd been with them in Central Park. And that spook Jonah had abducted him.

Jonah didn't abduct me.

This was creepy. Alex wasn't aware of trying to communicate what he was thinking. The guy apparently could read minds now. How could he mask his own thoughts?

There's nothing you can do about this, Alex. What you are thinking, and what you want others to know, it's all the same here. There are no secrets. We are in complete communication.

Geez, the poor slob had been absorbed. *Why did you let Jonah take you away? Why didn't you fight him?*

Fighting doesn't exist here.

But you're one of us—you're a human being! At least, you used to be a human being. I don't know what you are now.

I chose to go with Jonah, to come here.

Why?

He offered me something I didn't have on Earth.

You're talking in riddles, man. You got nothing here. You got no food, no clothes. . . . Geez, you don't even have a face!

Did I have a face on Earth?

What are you talking about?

Do you remember my face, Alex? Tell me about my face, describe it to me. My nose, was it straight or crooked? My ears, did they stick out? What color hair did I have? What color were my eyes?

How the hell should I know? I hardly knew you.

Exactly. You didn't know me at all. Nobody knew me. I didn't belong anywhere. I tried to be a buddy, I tried to be a rebel. Nothing worked for me. Here, everyone knows me, I know everyone. We are bound and committed to each other. Here, I belong.

Alex tried to absorb his attitude. It didn't make any more sense here than it would have made on Earth. *You're crazy, man. Who wants to belong here? Who wants to belong anywhere? Where's your self-respect? No one belongs to anyone, we're all on our own. You can't rely on anyone in this world, pal.*

Not in your world, Alex. In this world, we belong to each other.

And you like this? You like just hanging out like this, doing nothing?

What did I do on Earth that was so important? What did you do?

Alex's frustration level was rising. *You're nothing here, man! You're not even real!*

Oh, yes, I am real. More real than ever. Because I'm not alone. I'm part of something. This is unity. This is power.

Power? You can't even throw a punch!

Real power, Alex. Power beyond your comprehension. The kind of power that could remove the entire population from the face of the Earth.

Another "voice" joined them. *How did they do that, Adam? Do you know?*

It was Shalini. Alex had forgotten that she was there with him.

Am I so easy to forget, Alex?

He was going to have to be more careful about what he was thinking.

I understand, Alex. I understand what Adam tells us. I, too, have never felt attached, except to my family. You were my first friend, Alex. But you don't really know me at all. Even my parents didn't know me, not really. Adam, tell me about the power you have now, the power in belonging.

It's the energy of spirits, Shalini, millions of spirits, who make no judgments about each other.

They are in complete and total synchronization. The strength of a cosmic spirit is stronger than any physical force on Earth. This is the unity of intelligence, of cooperation.

Adam's words were getting creepier and creepier. *Shalini, we have to get out of here.*

No, Alex. This is the adventure. This is what I've wanted ever since we found the imprint of the spaceship.

There was no spaceship. That was Adam speaking.

Alex hastened to argue this. *I saw it too.*

It was a visual deception. They tricked your eyes. Because they knew we couldn't comprehend without seeing something. They knew we wouldn't come looking for them without physical evidence of their existence.

Alex was startled. *They wanted us to come looking for them? Why? No, wait, I get it. They left us behind, by accident, and this was a way to trap us.*

No, Alex. They didn't leave us behind by accident. And they don't want to trap us. They want to save us. They want to save themselves.

Jake was trying very hard to understand what Jonah was telling him.

Thousands of years . . . thousands of years without feeling. Without music, without art. Years without books, without learning. Without the warmth of the sun, without the smell of the flowers. Without love. After a few seconds, he added, *Without chocolate.*

How do you know these things exist?

This is our curse. There is this memory.

The magnitude of what Jonah was telling him was enormous, and the knowledge of what these spirits missed was horrifying. But there were implications for him and for his fellow human beings that were even more terrifying.

Because now he thought he knew why the population of Earth had been brought there and what was going to happen to them all.

You want to have bodies again. You want to have what you had thousands of years ago. You want to be able to experience feelings, all the sensations that humans can feel.

Yes.

You want our *bodies.*

Yes.

a word kept repeating itself in Kesha's consciousness over and over. Ecstasy. Had she ever used this word before? She didn't think so. She'd heard it, of course. In very different circumstances.

An old image, a memory . . . herself, as a little girl in church. People singing, joyful and weeping, a chorus of hallelujahs. A woman in the aisle, dancing wildly, her arms waving about as she cried out praises to the heavens. Mama, what's wrong with that lady, little Kesha asks. She is outside of herself, her mother replies. She is ecstatic.

The dopers at school . . . big Kesha in a rest room stall, overhearing a conversation. I was high for six hours, the girl says. I was on top of the world, I was flying, I had an out-of-body experience. It was wonderful. I guess that's why they call it Ecstasy.

But now Kesha knew the real meaning of the word. This is ecstasy, she thought. She was out of her body, she was light, she was free. It wasn't only the lack of a physical self that freed her. The fears, the worries and concerns, the goblins that plagued her . . . gone, all gone.

When her grandmother was disturbed about something, she used to say she had the weight of the world on her shoulders. Kesha used to know that feeling, too. When she read a newspaper or looked at a news report on television, all she saw were wars and riots, genocide, famine, detestation. People suffering at the hands of other people or through deadly illness or through disasters of nature. At those times, she felt the weight of the world on her shoulders. And ever since the Disappearance, she'd worried about the people who were gone, and the ones left behind.

But that weight couldn't touch her now. There was no genocide, no famine here. She had no cares at all.

She was alone and yet not alone. She knew the others who had walked the path of the labyrinth were there with her, but she didn't feel the need to cling to them. She wanted to move on, to experience this new world and to know it completely. She'd never thought of herself as someone who could adjust to new and unfamiliar places easily and readily. But this world, the peaceful world, was already so very comfortable.

Yes, it is *comfortable here.*

Instinctively, she knew she'd been addressed by a stranger. And it occurred to her that meeting others here would be very different from meeting people on Earth. Without a face, a presence, she couldn't make any assessment of this stranger. She couldn't have any assumptions. At this very moment, she had no idea what kind of being had addressed her.

She didn't intend to be rude, but there was something she wanted to know right off. So in her usual blunt, straightforward, no-bull manner, she asked: *Are you a native here? Or are you someone from Earth?*

She hoped her direct approach wouldn't be a turnoff to this being. Apparently, it wasn't.

I'm from Earth. You too, right?

How could you tell?

You have a personality. The natives here are pretty bland. Not hostile or anything. Just bland. Dull as dishwater, actually.

So this was a human. But it was odd, knowing nothing else about this contact she had made. She realized how important visual clues were, how much they told you about someone. Here, you wouldn't receive any sort of immediate impression, and you couldn't make one either. At this very moment, she didn't know how old this person was, if he or she was white or black or even male or female. How could she address this person without knowing these things?

And this other person knew nothing about her, either. How bizarre . . . but how liberating! There were millions of questions she could ask. The answers would give her a way to place this person in a category, get some sort of a handle on him or her. But then she'd have to come clean, too. She tried to think of a way to continue the conversation without getting into anything that might trap either of them into revealing personal characteristics.

Have you been here long?

Haven't we all?

No, actually, I just arrived. I'm with a group that was left behind on Earth.

Oh.

Was it frightening when you were brought here?

It was pretty weird. One minute, I was walking down a street, headed toward a hot dog stand to get some lunch. Then, the next thing I knew, there was this—this something, sort of in the shape of a human being but definitely not a human being. All around me, people started screaming. It only lasted a second.

Was it one of them? One of the natives? I thought they didn't have any form.

They don't. They were able to create some sort of image of what they thought a human being looked like—so we wouldn't freak when we saw them. Only they underestimated the size and confused a lot of body parts, too. The thing I saw had arms longer than his legs and ears the size of basketballs. Plus, the mouth and the nose were reversed.

Kesha couldn't help herself. The image sounded more funny than terrifying. She must have communicated her urge to laugh, but fortunately, he wasn't offended.

Yeah, I guess it does sound pretty funny now. But I can guarantee you, we weren't exactly chuckling at the time.

So the person had a sense of humor. That was interesting.

What happened next?

We were here.

What happened to your bodies?

We were informed that they were in good shape, but human bodies can't survive in this atmosphere so they're being stored somewhere. I'm picturing some sort of gigantic warehouse. I just hope they have a better system than my dry cleaner's. The last time I gave them a receipt I got someone else's blue blazer. I wouldn't want to go back to Earth in someone else's body.

No, that wouldn't be too cool . . . So, you think you're going back?

Yeah, I'm an optimist.

Are you afraid?

No. It's impossible to be afraid here. There's nothing to be afraid of.

Exactly, Kesha thought. That was what she liked about it. She must have communicated that, because her new friend replied.

Nice in some ways. Not in all ways.

She didn't want to hear about the not-nice ways now. She was enjoying herself; she was enjoying this conversation. Of course, they weren't actually speaking, and there wasn't any language involved. Which made this exchange even more interesting. She was picking up some clues about the person, too—that remark about lunch. Was New York the only city that had hot dog stands on street corners? And what about the blue blazer . . . did that mean he was a he? No, girls wore blazers, too.

Anyway, who cared? She had a companion, an interesting, witty friend. That was all that mattered now.

It was all making sense, Jake thought. Everything Jonah told him, as incredible as it seemed, was totally logical. Jake tried to commit it all to memory, to record in his journal. If he ever saw the journal again.

We were aware of your world. We knew what was happening there. At one point, we assumed you were going to evolve as we had. Your environment was deteriorating. Your bodies were weakening. You had not begun to compensate with an increase in cerebral power, but we assumed this would come eventually.

Then there were developments we did not antic-ipate. Humans began to take notice of the environ-ment. There was an improvement in the health of their bodies.

Yet your spiritual weakness continued and did not improve. You were unable to care for your-selves and one another as a united species. You were unable to live together peacefully. Chemicals were used to blunt sensations. Youth was not prop-erly nurtured. There was war, hunger, a lack of shelter and protection, unnecessary competitions for power.

Here, we have peace. We have equality. We have no suffering. But we also have no sensation, no feeling. You had sensations, you had emotional ca-pability, but you abused it. You were able to love, but you withheld love. You were capable of reason, but you allowed emotion to rule when reason should govern.

What followed was a condemnation of humanity, its inadequacies and its foibles and misjudgments throughout the history of civilization. Jake had heard it all before in a hundred sci-fi movies that involved an alien population attempting a takeover of the world. He was reminded, too, of a French exchange student at Madison, who incessantly dis-paraged American ways and customs—from our culture to our politics to the way we handled a knife and fork. It was boring then, and this was boring now. And just as he never got into an argument with the French student over the American system, he didn't think this was the time or the place to attempt a defense of humanity.

What Jonah's diatribe boiled down to was this: humans didn't take advantage of their gifts, thus, they didn't deserve them.

We wanted your bodies. We decided to live on Earth in your bodies. We knew we could make better use of them. So we took them.

Jake had to get a word in here.

Why didn't you take the fifth period geometry class at Madison High along with everyone else?

We decided to leave an interesting group intact, so that we could observe modes of communication and interaction. Your group represented a variety of so-called personality types, as well as all major racial and ethnic identities. We decided to leave you on Earth so that we could study your mannerisms, until such a time that we no longer needed instruction.

So glad we ould help out, Jake thought sarcastically, and then remembered how easy it was for them to read minds. Well, it didn't matter. Jonah wouldn't have any comprehension of sarcasm.

He thought of another question that had been bugging him for a long time.

The animals . . . there were animals all over the place just after the people disappeared. Then the animals disappeared. Why didn't you take the animals at the same time?

We had no interest in nonhuman species. We re-

moved them when we realized they were not capable of caring for themselves. They have been placed safely in a state of suspended animation.

So you were watching us down there on Earth.

Yes.

All the time.

Yes.

Jake recalled a number of times when he had been alone with Ashley. If he could blush in this condition now, he would.

I hope you learned a lot.

We did.

So why aren't you all down there in our bodies now?

For a moment, he thought he'd lost Jonah's attention. Finally, Jonah replied.

Since you did not have our mental capabilities, we assumed that once we separated the consciousness of humanity from its physical form, the human consciousness would rapidly deteriorate. We believed you could not survive without the powers that were only available through your physical presence.

Jake translated this. *You figured we'd be nothing without our looks or the ability to fight.*

Yes. We underestimated the human consciousness. We were not cognizant of independent spirit, emotional fortitude, strength of character. Individuality, personality, these were aspects of consciousness that we did not take into consideration.

So our human consciousness survived.

Yes.

So humans weren't so completely lousy after all. But that didn't guarantee them a future.

You have the power here. Why haven't you just destroyed our consciousness and taken over the bodies?

We do not destroy. We are incapable of destruction. We learned the consequences of destruction, and this will not happen again. We developed an alternate plan.

These guys didn't give up easily, Jake thought. He couldn't wait to hear what new thrills they'd dreamed up for the human species.

What was the plan?

We would simply exchange places. Your spirits would continue to exist here, where you do no harm without your bodies—not to the environment or your fellow human beings. You would be incapable of aggression. It would be thousands, perhaps millions of years before your individual personalities and layers of consciousness would unite, providing you with any significant power in the world. And with your bodies, we would inherit the Earth.

So why haven't you done that?

We tried. I proposed myself for the first experiment. I selected a body at random from storage.

Yeah, I remember what you looked like.

Do you remember anything else about me? What was your assessment of my character?

Jake couldn't think of a thing to say. Jonah had been pretty much a blob. He didn't want to say that, but he remembered too late that Jonah could read his mind.

A blob, something of no substance. I made no impact on Earth. With the loss of sensation, we lost all elements of personality and individuality. We are completely in accord, agreement, and synchro-

nization. There is nothing to divide us.

But you took over some bodies for a while.

Yes. Those particular bodies lacked strength of character and were easy to absorb.

Alex, Shalini, and David, Jake remembered. Yes, he could understand that. Jonah continued.

But this only confirmed what we had come to suspect. We could exist, but we could not function on Earth. We cannot create, we cannot build. The physical ability to experience the five senses does not automatically result in the ability to feel in a spiritual or emotional manner. Perhaps, in time, in thousands or millions of years, this could develop. But your bodies were not designed to survive that long, despite whatever care is taken in their maintenance. And we would not be able to develop sufficient emotion to enter into the relationship necessary for procreation. With the deterioration of the human bodies we occupied, all would be finished. We would cease to exist.

Jake didn't know what to say. He couldn't feel sorry for the spirit—after all, its plan involved the end of human consciousness. But this spirit consciousness would die too. Jonah, for once, misunderstood his silence.

I realize that you may not have the intellectual capacity to comprehend all that I have told you. Perhaps an illustration will help you to understand the situation. I can provide you with the ability to witness our attempts to function on Earth.

Okay.

Look.

Jake looked. And he saw . . . himself. Sort of.

*   *   *

It was lonely now, with everyone gone, Ashley thought. She would have liked to have gone with the others, but she'd made a promise. She just hoped that Jake would return safely. And bring her dear friend Corey back with him. Not to mention the rest of the human race.

Of course, not *everyone* was gone. Cam was here and Charlotte. But they seemed to have developed some sort of private *thing*, a friendship or communication or something that seemed almost intimate. Ashley knew that if she approached them, they wouldn't be unfriendly. But she didn't want to disturb whatever was going on between them.

Was it really possible that Cam had found a soul mate? He was so odd . . . but then, so was Charlotte. Maybe it was fate that brought them together.

She wondered if it was fate that had brought her and Jake together. She wasn't even sure if she believed in fate—or destiny or any of that New Age stuff. All she knew was that when she was with Jake, she felt whole, she felt real. She missed that feeling right now.

She and Cam and Charlotte weren't the only beings on Earth. The aliens were around, hanging out in their human forms. It was strange to see someone who looked exactly like Kesha staring at herself in a mirror for hours. It just wasn't a Kesha sort of thing to do.

The others were exploring the world of sensation in different ways. She could see the David alien and the Martina alien in the orchard, smelling fruit. Several of them were in the swimming pool. They couldn't swim, but they seemed content to feel the cold wetness under the hot California sun and some sort of survival instinct kept them from drowning. The un-Travis was still in the kitchen, eating. Taste seemed to be the only sense he really desired.

Or was that the right word? Could these creatures feel desires? Did they wish for things, did they want stuff? Did they long for anything? From what she'd understood, she didn't think so.

She went into the kitchen. The un-Travis said nothing to her. He was steadfastly working his way through a pint of Häagen-Dazs chocolate chocolate chip. She poured herself a soda, and filled the glass liberally with ice. Then she went back outside.

What was really strange was seeing the body of Jake there, flat on its back, stark naked. He was motionless. After a few seconds, she became alarmed. She didn't want this alien leaving Jake with a nasty sunburn.

She approached him. "You shouldn't do this. It's not healthy."

He looked at her. "The sensation of heat absorbed in this manner does not cause what a human body construes as pain."

She averted her eyes. Knowing this wasn't really Jake made the sight feel . . . uncomfortable. "It may not hurt right now," Ashley said, "but it will later." She picked his clothes up off the ground and tossed them to him. "Put this on."

He did as he was told, which only served to emphasize the fact that he was not Jake.

"Did you like the sensation of heat?" she asked him.

"Like?" he repeated.

"Enjoy. Take pleasure from. Appreciate."

"I know the meaning of the word," he said,

"but I have not developed the awareness of it."

"Oh." She took an ice cube out of her soda. "This is cold. It's the opposite of hot." She placed it in his hand. He held it there and examined it. After a few seconds, a trickle of water ran down his arm.

"It is changing its form," he noted, "from solid to liquid."

She nodded. "That's called melting." She hoped he wouldn't ask her for a real chemical explanation of the procedure.

She had nothing to worry about. "I know this," the un-Jake said. "I am simply commenting on the experience of observing the actual molecular activity for the first time."

"Right," Ashley said. She looked around to see if there was something else she could demonstrate to him. She picked up a rock. "This is hard."

He accepted it, acknowledged its hardness, and dropped it.

Ashley picked a dandelion off the grass. "This is soft." She blew the feathery tufts into the air.

They walked around the house together. Ashley kept her eyes open for anything that would serve as an example for a sensation. A mirror provided the experience of smooth. On some half-built bookcases, she discovered a bit of sandpaper.

"Rough," she said.

He felt it. "Rough," he repeated. Then he touched his cheek. Jake was in need of a shave.

"Rough," he said again. He reached over and touched her cheek. "Smooth."

The gesture gave her a funny feeling. Jake used to touch her right there.

"Art," she said suddenly. "You should see some art while you're here."

Unfortunately, the house itself didn't contain many works of art. But Ashley located a big coffee-table book *Paintings from the Metropolitan Museum of Art*, and she opened it.

The pictures of paintings in the book weren't like the paintings themselves, but it was better than nothing. "This is Monet," she said, pointing to one. "He's my favorite artist." She knew words like "favorite" couldn't have any meaning to him, but what the hell. Maybe they would encourage him to look at the work critically.

It didn't seem likely that he was going to develop an appreciation of art right away. He stared at each picture without comment or expression. Every now and then he would point to a spot on the painting and say, "red" or "yellow." Identifying colors seemed to be his only way of relating to the work.

"Let's try music," she said. She took him to the living room, where there was a stereo system. "We'll start with classical." She selected Pachelbel's Canon in D and put the disc into the player. The sweet, wistful notes filled the room. She looked at the un-Jake. Nothing.

After a while, she stopped the CD. "Okay, let's go with rock." For this, she had a harder time making a selection. Classic rock, like the Rolling Stones? Something more contemporary? Metal, acid, punk? House?

She settled on a greatest-hits-of-the-nineties compilation and stuck it into the player. The first number on the disc was Madonna. The un-Jake winced.

"I'm not that crazy about her either," Ashley confessed. Then she realized that Jake's—the un-Jake's expression had nothing to do with the music. He was examining his hand.

Ashley looked. "Oh, you cut yourself. It hurts, huh?"

"This is the sensation of pain," the un-Jake said.

"Right," Ashley said. "Come with me." She led him to a bathroom, where she applied a bit of antiseptic ointment and a Band-Aid. "It might sting for a while, but it will feel better soon."

He didn't thank her, but she doubted that courtesy was an aspect of their culture. "Did your—" she stopped. She didn't want to say "species"— that sounded so cold. "Your people—did they ever have anything like this? Music, art . . ."

"Yes," the un-Jake said, "thousands of years ago. There is a dim collective memory."

"Oh." She looked at him curiously. The aliens claimed to feel no emotion. But she could have sworn she detected a note of sadness in his voice.

seven

it didn't take long for Alex to give up on Adam. Obviously, his ex-classmate had been through some sort of mind game and been indoctrinated into believing his captors were his friends. Alex had read about this, it was the something-or-other syndrome, where victims became so dependent that they switched sides and joined up with the bad guys. It was clear that Adam had gone over the edge and could now be categorized as essentially brain-dead.

This place was giving him the creeps, but he wasn't abandoning his rescue mission. It was too late to save Adam, but surely there were plenty of humans left to make a rebellion. He called for Shalini.

There was no response.

Shalini?

She wasn't there.

He started to panic. *What have you bastards done to her?*

Chill out, Popov. No one's done anything to her. That was loverboy speaking. His words were no comfort. David Chu was just the kind of guy who could have abducted her.

Where is she? Alex demanded.

She's hanging out—she's getting to know the natives. Man, you really keep her on a short leash.

Yeah, well, maybe she needs protection from sex maniacs.

I don't think you'll find a lot of sex maniacs up here, Popov. Maybe you haven't noticed, but they're not exactly what you'd call a physical bunch.

I'm not talking about the natives.

Oh, I get it. You think I'll put the moves on her. You did before.

Desperation, man.

Alex didn't know where to focus his anger—in defense of Shalini's desirability or in continuing to attack David's character. He chose the latter.

You're such a sleaze, Chu. You don't care about anyone. You just keep hitting on chicks till they give in, then you dump them.

Yeah? Well, at least I don't try to own them.

What the hell's that supposed to mean?

You telling me you don't treat Shalini like she's something you bought at the pet store?

A new "voice" entered the conversation. *Cease your argument. You are disrupting our world.*

Alex sneered. *Maybe your world could use a little disruption, spook. This place is pretty deadly.*

The spook replied. *This place is peaceful. We have no arguments, no confrontations here. We live together in complete cooperation. You will not bring disharmony to our world.*

It was David's turn to rebut. *Like you guys didn't create any disharmony in our world?*

Your world is by nature disharmonious. You are

in a constant state of battle. We have no interest in this.

It wasn't easy to appear threatening when you had no tone of voice, no expression to back it up. But Alex did his best. *Maybe you'd better start drumming up some interest, pal. Come on, Chu, let's go.*

Let's go where? We don't have any feet, in case you haven't noticed.

Just stay with me, stupid.

Why? You scared to be alone?

Alex wished he could strangle the jerk right then and there. But he couldn't afford to lose any humans. Not to mention the fact that he had no hands. *No, I'm not scared. But did you see Adam? They got into his head; he's been brainwashed. We gotta see if we can get people out of here before they're all turned into zombies.*

How do you figure on doing that? You got some secret plan for exterminating the spooks? We can't even see them!

Forget extermination. We have to concentrate on getting the humans out.

What's this "we" crap? What makes you think I'm going to help you?

You're the playboy, man. Are you going to be content with, what, a dozen girls on the face of the Earth?

The lack of response to this was a pretty good indication that Alex had hit on a very sensitive issue. David spoke.

You got any ideas how we go about arranging this great escape?

As it happened, Alex didn't have any ideas, but

he continued as if it were all arranged. *Yeah, but we need to find some humans first. Then we can start getting them organized.* He concentrated on the potential of telepathic communication and issued a general question.

Is anyone out there who can hear me? He quickly amended that. *Anyone human?*

There was a response. *We are human.*

Who are you? Where are you from? How did you get here?

It was clear David didn't approve of Alex's interviewing methods. *Geez, Popov, give them a break. This isn't the Spanish inquisition.*

But the humans didn't appear to have any problems in responding immediately to Alex's interrogation.

We came from Paris. We are fifteen French girls between the ages of seventeen and twenty-two. We were all on the runway of a fashion show in Paris when we were taken away.

Alex knew David had to be in seventh heaven. Fifteen French fashion models. Alex would have preferred a squadron of Marines, but Don Juan had lucked out.

And now David joined in the interrogation. *What do you look like?*

We look like nothing now.

What did you look like before?

We were all tall.

David made a special plea. *Don't use the past tense. We're all going to get back to the way we were. Think of being on that Paris runway and describe yourselves to me.*

The spokesperson for the models obliged. *We*

are six blondes, seven brunettes, two redheads. Three of us are black, four of us are Asians. Eight of us have brown eyes. Five of us have blue eyes. Two of us have green eyes. Five of us have toenails painted red. Three of us wear contact lenses. One of us has a tattoo of a rose on her left shoulder. Two of us have a small scar resulting from appendix removal. One of us has a birthmark on the right thigh. Four of us—

Apparently, David didn't need that much detail. *Okay, okay, I get the picture. The main thing is, you're all beautiful, right?*

We have all been determined beautiful by human earthly standards.

What other standards are there? The yokels around here, they could be ugly as sin for all we know. Man, you babes must be unbelievably gorgeous.

Ugly, beautiful, gorgeous—these words have no meaning here.

Well, they got plenty of meaning where I come from. And I know you've got words that mean the same thing in French.

We are none of us like that anymore.

Not here, maybe. But don't worry, doll, once you're back where you belong, you'll all be babes again.

Alex decided it was time to get the subject moving in a more intelligent and useful direction. *It's good that you know English. We need to discuss something serious.*

We have very little knowledge of English.

Sure you do—you're talking just fine. You understand us, we understand you, right? And I'm not speaking French—I don't know any French. You speak French, Chu?

Not a word. I speak the universal language.

What's that?

The language of love. You girls can speak that too, right?

Alex ignored that and addressed the girls. *Don't listen to him. Keep speaking in English—you're doing fine.*

The models corrected him. *There is no language here. We can all communicate now, no matter what language we spoke before. Nationality, ethnicity, they mean nothing here, just as physical appearance means nothing. Race means nothing. Sex means nothing.*

Even without any voice, David managed to convey a sense of outrage. *Don't talk like that! This is sick!*

Alex took over. *We want to get you all out of here. We're trying to organize something. There has to be a way we can fight them off and escape. You've been here longer than we have—do you know what their weaknesses are?*

We have no wish to fight.

Yeah, I can deal with that. You're girls—you're not used to real aggression. Don't worry; we'll handle that and we'll take care of you. Just tell us what you know about these spooks.

We are not in need of your protection. Here, we are all equal. What was male and female are one. We have no desire to fight.

How else are you going to get out of here?

We have no desire to leave.

Alex absorbed the words in horror. *Ohmigod,*

they're zombies too. They're just like Adam—they've been brainwashed.

We are not zombies. We have evolved. We have achieved a higher level of awareness. We are aware of the superficiality of our previous meaningless lives. We have understanding now. We are one with the universe.

The anguish and despair in David's response was so strong, Alex could practically hear it. *Popov, do you hear that? Those are models talking! I'm gonna kill these spokes!*

Have you ever wondered, Kesha said, *why people always look straight ahead in elevators?*

That one's easy, Corey replied. *They're in a confined space with total strangers and they don't want to encourage any intimacy. How about this one? A person goes to the elevator in a building. Other people are standing there. But the new person pushes the button again, even though it's clear that the others are also waiting for the elevator, Why?*

Kesha answered immediately. *Because the new person doesn't trust the other people to be smart enough to have pushed the button.*

But the button is lit, indicating that the elevator has been called. Why does the new person push it again?

Kesha considered the implication of this. *Because . . . because he doesn't trust his own sight?*

Not bad. How about because he wants to make sure the others know why he's standing there? So they won't think he's joined them for another reason, like trying to make their acquaintance?

Kesha wished she could laugh, to show Corey how much she enjoyed his comment. But she suspected he knew that she appreciated his wit by now. They'd been going on like this for who knew how long, exchanging their views on general human silliness. It was amazing how in synch they were! They'd analyzed and examined the way people cannot pass a mirror or a reflective window without checking out their appearance. And they'd had a long discussion of behavior on subways—how strangers will not make eye contact unless a nut comes into the car and starts screaming about how the end of the world is coming or something like that. Then the strangers immediately begin exchanging looks of complicity, as if to say, he's crazy, we're sane. Which when you thought about it, given their current circumstances, was ironic.

The discussion of subways confirmed that Kesha's new friend was from New York. She also knew her friend's name: Corey. But a name like that didn't tell her if this was a boy or a girl she was speaking to.

Corey had to know more about her now than she knew about him. He—or she—knew she was from New York. A slip of her tongue clued him in to the fact that she was a senior in high school. He probably guessed that she was a girl—the name Kesha had a distinctly feminine sound. Since the name had an African derivation, he might also have concluded that she was black.

She did know something about Corey. He or she had an excellent sense of humor, a warm personality, a keen eye for the wackiness of people but a general love of humanity, too. Corey seemed to be interested in everything and didn't seem to have any "isms," like sexism or racism or ageism—at least, he—or she—hadn't demonstrated a belief in any stereotypes.

Funny, how she kept envisioning Corey as a he. Nothing that had been said gave any indication of that. People frequently used the pronoun "he" when talking about a person whose sex wasn't known, like an unborn baby. But Kesha had always considered that habit to be inherently sexist, and she usually avoided falling into that trap.

But he or she, one thing was clear—this Corey was a beautiful person. And a friend. A close friend, despite the fact that she'd only known him/her for—how long? She had absolutely no idea. Time seemed to be of no consequence here. It just wasn't relevant to the way they were living. Without the need to eat, to drink or sleep or even pee, with no chores or routines, there was nothing to break up the time, to divide it into parts of the day. They had nothing to do but communicate, to get to know each other—and that was fine by her.

She spoke impulsively. *You know what I like best about being here?*

What?

Having no responsibilities. Back in New York, it always seemed like I had to be somewhere, I had something to do, and I was always late.

I know what you mean. I think I spent half my life looking at my watch.

You know what else I like?

What?

Being weightless and light. I used to feel like I was so big. I wasn't fat, really, just big. Tall, with big feet and big hands and broad shoulders for a girl. I always felt like I took up so much space.

I doubt that you ever took up any more space than you needed.

She loved when Corey said things like that. *Well, like I said, for a girl.*

Is there some sort of size standard for girls that I'm not aware of?

Oh, come on, you know what I mean. Of course there are standards. Girls want to be smaller than guys; guys want to be bigger than girls. Right?

I guess that's the tradition. But I work with a lot of models, female models, and they have to be taller than most of the men they know. Yet, they're still considered the epitome of beauty.

Are you a model?

No, I photograph models.

Kesha decided that if Corey turned out to be a guy, she could forget about appealing to him.

You must see a lot of beautiful women every day.

Beauty is in the eye of the beholder. Corny, but true. Everyone can be beautiful in his or her own way.

Oh, if only that were true and not just some idealistic philosophy that everyone proclaimed and no one really believed. She wouldn't let him get away with this.

That's bull. Physical appearance is still important. I guess it has something to do with the way people try to attract each other. For romance. Guys want to look good so girls will like them—girls want to look good for guys. Unless they're gay, of course. But it's still the same thing. The first thing one person notices about another person is the way that person looks. That's another thing I like about being here. No one can tell what anyone else looks like.

She felt like she'd just given a very personal lecture, and she felt stupid. Now he would assume that she was not a pretty girl. Maybe that was just as well.

But he still wanted to continue the discussion.

Sight is a powerful sense. But not all people see things the same way. Beauty is subjective. Some people think the work of Picasso is beautiful—some people think it's ugly. All people do not find the same sights appealing. Life would be pretty boring if they did. Like life here. It would be impossible to make any real or lasting relationships.

Kesha was incredulous. *You think life here is lousy for relationships?*

Don't you?

No! I think—I think it's wonderful. Nobody's making any judgments or comparisons. Did she dare? Why not? *Like, I don't even know if you're a male or a female.*

Would it make any difference to you?

No.

Of course it would. Depending on your sexual orientation.

I'm heterosexual. But that's not relevant. People should become friends first, before they even think about another kind of relationship! I think it's good not to know someone's sex or how they look or anything like that when you first meet someone. We should concentrate on who a person is and whether or not we can be friends with each other.

He had an answer for that. *But we're already*

friends, aren't we? So now we can move on. If we want to.

Kesha could have sworn she had a body, and it was trembling. *What do you mean?*

I'm a twenty-four-year-old heterosexual male. You're a—how old?

Eighteen.

Eighteen-year-old-heterosexual female. I'd say there were some possibilities here. If we were back on Earth.

In other words, if they had bodies and faces, she thought. But how would he feel about her then?

She wasn't sure she wanted to know. Because she was already in love with this guy.

eight

Jake was thinking about how one's perspective could change when you saw something up close.

Actually, that wasn't accurate. He probably shouldn't think that way when he couldn't see anything at all. He reworked the notion and came up with a traditional saying: you can't know a man until you've walked a mile in his shoes. As a writer for his school's newspaper and therefore mindful of the need to be politically correct, he amended that to "you can't know a person until you've walked a mile in his or her shoes."

Only now his literary sensibilities were offended. That his-or-her business was awkward. Usually he dealt with problems like this by converting to the plural; in other words, you can't know people until you've walked a mile in their shoes. But no, that stunk; it gave the impression of walking in a hundred pairs of shoes at the same time.

If he'd had a head, he would have shaken it right then and there to pull himself out of this ridiculous argument in semantics. But what else was there to do here but ponder the tiniest of issues and concerns? All the big stuff—wars, plagues, natural disasters—were taken care of. There were no wrongs to be made right, no problems to solve. No actions were needed. There was all the time in the world to think.

That was a good thing, because he'd had time to learn something about this place and its inhabitants. They weren't the enemy. At least, it was impossible for him to perceive them in this way anymore. Okay, sure, maybe it wasn't very nice of them to abduct practically the entire population of Earth in an attempt to use their bodies. But he couldn't blame them for trying to get their hands on some *real* bodies. It was a wretched irony for them that they could have the bodies, they could take them so easily, but they couldn't live in them. Bad news for the aliens. Good news for the residents of the planet Earth. If the aliens would simply let them all go.

Only now, he had another problem. Having been here for a while, having existed as they did, having walked in their—metaphoric—shoes, he cared about what happened to these beings. But there was nothing he could do for them.

He realized that Jonah was there with him. As usual, the spirit was able to read his thoughts.

There is something you can do for us.

What?

It is difficult to explain to a human. You are not capable of this level of comprehension.

Jonah expressed this simply and without any arrogance, but his constant assumption of the superiority of his species was beginning to bug Jake, and he couldn't resist making this known.

If I'm too feebleminded to understand what I can

do for you, then I doubt that I'll be able to do it.

Jonah, naturally, was oblivious of the sarcasm.

It is my belief that a visual presentation will be more convincing to you than a purely intellectual explanation. This would be in keeping with the limited perspective available to you, the dependence on physical sensation that is inherent to your species.

Jake was losing his patience.

Okay, okay, I get it. Show me.

Observe.

It wasn't exactly like seeing—more like a visual imprint on his brain. It was as if he were seeing a movie inside of his head.

There was the farm, outside Los Angeles. Charlotte was there, alone. Apparently, she had just come from the orchard, because she carried a basket of fruit. From what Jake could make out, they looked like peaches, maybe nectarines. She took one out of the basket and bit into it. The expression on her face made it clear that the fruit was delicious. She ate it slowly, savoring every bite. The rapture on her face was remarkable. Jake himself liked a good, ripe peach, but he didn't think he'd ever enjoyed one quite that much.

Jonah responded to his thoughts.

She can appreciate the fruit in a way that is far beyond the average capability of human beings. By accepting our spirit, she has achieved a higher level of awareness. This is what we have given her.

Jake tried to make sense of this.

So, she lets you live inside her head and you give her sharper taste buds. I don't know if I'd call that a fair trade.

She can appreciate all sensual experiences in a more profound way. Her connection to the world around her extends to everything. Observe how she shares her fruit.

Now Charlotte approached the swimming pool, where all the aliens on Earth were gathered. She offered a piece of fruit to each one. Personally, Jake didn't think this was such an amazing gesture, and he pointed this out to Jonah.

Humans can be generous without having alien spirits embedded in their consciousnesses.

But do they actually desire that all others share in the pleasure? Humans must be trained to behave in that way. It is what you call manners. You are taught to share. For us, this is instinctive, because we are connected. Do you understand the difference?

Okay, I get it. What's your point? What do you want?

A merger. Our spirit combined with the consciousness of humanity. We will have the ability to know physical sensation. You will have the ability to live in harmony with all of creation. Would you call that a fair trade?

Ashley thought that the body of Jake now ran like the real Jake, with the same long strides, the same swing of his arms. He even clenched his fists like Jake did when he ran.

She recalled how the alien had moved when he first arrived in Jake's body. His pace had been awkward, his motions clumsy and jerky. He was becoming adjusted to having a body much more quickly than the others were. From where she was standing, watching the form of her boyfriend run around the perimeter of the labyrinth, she could almost believe that he was really and truly Jake.

She waved at him. He saw this, and came running toward her. Unfortunately, he hadn't learned to slow down to a gradual halt, and he stopped running too abruptly just a few steps in front of her. As he result, he lost his balance and toppled over, landing at her feet.

She couldn't help herself. She burst out laughing. He looked up from his position on the grass. "What I have done, falling, this is considered to be amusing to you?"

There was no reproach in his tone, but she was instantly ashamed. "No, I'm sorry—it's not funny at all."

"But laughter is the human response to comic behavior."

"Yeah, but something can look funny without actually being funny." She realized it was hopeless to attempt an explanation. There were elements of human nature that were simply beyond the comprehension of these beings. They could *know*, but they couldn't *understand*.

The un-Jake got to his feet. She noticed he was favoring a leg. "Did you hurt yourself when you fell?"

"How would I know this?"

"You'd probably feel some pain."

"Pain." He considered this. She hoped he wasn't about to ask her for an explanation of pain. Fortunately, whatever had weakened his leg appeared to be nothing more than a fleeting twinge. He wore no expression of discomfort.

"It must be amazing," she said, "to feel sensation when you haven't experienced it before. Like right now, after running so hard, you could be tired. Or you could be feeling invigorated."

He looked at her blankly.

"Jake was always full of energy after a run," she went on. "I couldn't understand why he wasn't exhausted. I know I would be."

His expression remained—expressionless. She knew he could hear what she was saying, and he could probably supply a dictionary definition of every word she had used. But would he ever be able to express the feelings that lay behind the words? Or even understand them? Given his current demeanor, this could take a long time.

It dawned on her that she was thinking of the un-Jake as if he were a real person. Or as if this were Jake himself, perhaps after an accident or illness and in need of major rehabilitation before he would be himself again.

She had to get this image out of her head. This wasn't Jake. But whoever he was, his temporary stay on Earth wouldn't be much fun if he couldn't appreciate any human sensations. She wanted to help him.

Gazing around the area, she wondered what else there was on the farm that he could be introduced to. He'd tasted the different fruits and vegetables, he'd smelled everything from roses to cow manure, and he'd heard all kinds of music, and looked at pictures of art. What else could she show him here?

But why stay here? It wasn't as if they were trapped in this one area. There weren't a lot of sights within walking distance, like there were in

New York, but Charlotte had demonstrated that it wasn't difficult to get around by car.

She could see Charlotte and Cam now, crouched down in the vegetable garden. They still seemed to be encased in that special glow of intimacy that kept Ashley from disturbing them. But right now, she had an idea that was too good to keep to herself. She grabbed the un-Jake's hand. "Come with me."

Neither Charlotte nor Cam appeared to be disturbed by their intrusion. Cam, of course, didn't even seem to notice them but continued to poke around some plant. Charlotte greeted them warmly. "What are you guys up to?"

"I've just had a brilliant idea," Ashley announced. "Let's go to Disneyland."

"Disneyland," Charlotte repeated.

"It's not far from here, is it?"

"No . . . but why do you want to go to Disneyland?"

"For the sensations! The rides, the sights, the animated characters! I'm trying to make Jake here get excited about something."

Cam looked up. "That's not Jake, Ashley."

"Yes, but you know who I mean," she said impatiently. "What do you think? Isn't this a great idea?"

Charlotte looked doubtful. "But there's no one there to operate the rides, and those animated characters won't be working."

"Cam could figure out how to make things work," Ashley said. "Couldn't you, Cam?"

"It depends," he said. "I guess it's possible."

Charlotte was interested. "Gosh, I haven't been

to Disneyland since I was a little kid." She turned to look toward the swimming pool. "Maybe we should get everyone together. I could take the bus."

But Cam disagreed. "Disneyland's a big experience. I've never been there, but my guess is that it's pretty overwhelming. It might be too much for them. And there are only three of us to take care of them all."

"That's a good point," Charlotte said. "The others seem content with what they're doing. They should be okay here. Let's do it!"

They piled into a small but sturdy Jeep, with Charlotte behind the wheel. Ashley sat in the backseat next to the un-Jake, who sat stiffly and stared straight ahead.

"What were you guys doing in the vegetable garden?" Ashley asked Cam and Charlotte.

"Deciding what to plant," Cam told her. "I'm thinking there's space for some brussels sprouts and asparagus. And I want to grow onions here."

He sounded like he was planning to be here for a while. Ashley's eyes darted between him and Charlotte. It seemed clear that something was going on, even though she hadn't witnessed any expression of physical affection. She tried to imagine Cam with Charlotte in the throes of passion, but it was impossible. Somehow, Cam didn't seem capable of showing any real demonstration of romance. It was like he always kept his feelings under lock and key. Or maybe he just couldn't have those kind of feelings.

Thank goodness, *she* could have those feelings. But that wasn't always such a good thing. Like right now, when she longed for her boyfriend to be back with her, safe and sound, holding her, making love . . .

"Have you ever been to Disneyland, Ashley?" Charlotte asked as she shifted gears to get the Jeep over a high curb. Ashley reached out to grip the un-Jake's arm to keep herself from tipping over, but she missed and grabbed his thigh instead. Quickly, she looked at him. He had no reaction to the unexpected and unintended intimacy.

She turned her attention to Charlotte's question. "No, I've never been to Disneyland."

"It's nice," Charlotte told her, "but not much when you compare it to Disney World in Florida."

"Well, I've never been there either," Ashley said. "So I'm sure I'll be impressed."

And she was. As she climbed over the turnstile to face the huge picture of Mickey Mouse created out of flowers, and saw the turrets of Sleeping Beauty's castle looming before her, she felt a real thrill.

She hoped the un-Jake was getting a kick out of this, too. "What do you think?" she asked him. "Isn't this wild? Have you ever seen anything like this before?"

Which was a very stupid question. How would the sights of Disneyland overwhelm someone who'd never experienced anything at all?

Charlotte was checking out a map display of the park. "Where do you want to go?" she asked. "Adventureland, Critter Country . . ."

Ashley joined her at the map. "Tomorrowland," she declared. Somehow, given their circumstances, it seemed appropriate.

The four of them wandered out into the vast expanse of the theme park. Ashley's eyes were as wide as any child's. She wished she could see some reaction in the un-Jake.

"It's so different without the crowds," Charlotte marveled. "You know what I remember most about coming here as a child? Standing in line."

There would be no lines today. They decided not to waste time trying to start up the monorail that could transport them quickly around the park. While the so-called "highway in the sky" might have been considered pretty spectacular in the 1950s when the park opened, today it didn't seem all that exciting.

But Tomorrowland still held breathtaking sensations for them. They were able to locate the station that held the control panels for the equipment, and Cam, with his usual technical genius, managed to figure out how to run the Astro Orbiter.

"The cars only hold two people," he noted. "I can't ride and work the controls at the same time. Charlotte, you want to ride in one of those things alone?"

"The three of us could squeeze into one car together," Ashley suggested, but Charlotte said she'd prefer to remain with Cam. "Besides," she said to Ashley, "I'm sure you'd prefer to be alone with Jake."

"Charlotte, this isn't Jake," Ashley reminded her, but Charlotte wasn't listening. She was watching Cam as he read the instructions on the panel and fiddled with the controls. Ashley had always been impressed with Cam's remarkable intellect, but she'd never looked at him quite like that.

The un-Jake said nothing as they got into the starship, and he allowed her to adjust his safety belt as if he were a child. "I have no idea what this ride is like," she told him, "and you might think it's pretty silly. You're supposed to feel like you're traveling through the solar system. It's mainly intended to give kids a big thrill."

Jake looked around the cramped space with mild interest. A soft humming sound indicated that Cam had gotten the thing started, and the ride was about to begin. That was the last soft sound they heard.

The Astro Orbiter had an amazing sound system—not just loud, but all encompassing. Having never been a passenger in a vehicle that could leave the planet Earth, Ashley had no way of knowing if the noise was authentic. But it certainly gave the effect of what she imagined a blastoff would be like.

Then, they were traveling through darkness, utter darkness. The speed at which they seemed to be moving was frightening. She grabbed Jake's hand. She couldn't see anything, but she knew her knuckles were turning white. As her eyes became accustomed to the dark, she found herself riveted by the sight she saw through the windows of the ship.

It reminded her of a scene from *Star Wars*. They moved through the cosmos, with planets and shooting stars and things that looked like flying saucers and spaceships all around them. Bright flashing lights and shrieking noises indicated intergalactic battles, fires, and explosions. After a few seconds, the trip ceased to be frightening and became actually thrilling, with visual and sound experiences unlike anything Ashley had ever experienced.

If it was all new and amazing to her, she couldn't imagine what it must be like for Jake. He said nothing, but when space explosions lit up the interior of their cabin she actually saw something like an expression on his face. She couldn't read it—but it was evident that he was feeling *something*.

Their orbit seemed to go on for a long time, and at one point Ashley wondered if Cam had discovered his romantic side. She feared that Cam and Charlotte had become so involved with each other that Cam had forgotten about them. But then the sensation of descending came over her, and the starship made a gentle landing.

At least, *she* thought it was gentle. The un-Jake appeared to be in a state of shock. Cam and Charlotte had to help her get him out of the craft. He was stiff with what Ashley suspected was fear.

"Are you okay?" she asked him anxiously.

Jake made some sounds, but he was incapable of speech. His whole body trembled, and he was gasping for breath.

"This is what I was afraid of," Cam said. "It was too much sensation for him to take in at once."

Ashley was frightened now. "What are we going to do? Is he going to be all right? Ohmigod, Cam, is he permanently damaged?"

"I'm not a doctor, Ashley," Cam said. He turned to Charlotte. "Do you know what's happening to him? Can you understand what he's feeling?"

Ashley had forgotten that Charlotte had the alien spirit within her. She was so normal, so real, so human. But Charlotte was looking at the un-Jake with compassion and concern that were almost beyond human.

"It has been too much for him," she acknowledged. "But it won't hurt him. He'll be okay."

But Jake—un-Jake—was still trembling and speechless. "What should we do?" Ashley asked her.

"Just walk around with him," Charlotte suggested. "Talk to him, explain it all to him. He's not stupid, Ashley, just . . . well, just a child. No, not even a child. Children have personalities. The alien in me, it brought a dimension to my consciousness, my feelings. But it had no real experience. Everything was new."

Ashley took his arm. "Can you walk?"

Stiffly, he took one step and then another. "Good, very good," Ashley said encouragingly. She turned back to Cam and Charlotte. "Where should we go? Back to the car?"

"Let him look around and get his bearings," Charlotte said. "Why don't we split up and meet back at the car in an hour?"

Ashley was about to tell her she didn't really want to be alone with Jake in this condition when she realized that what Charlotte really wanted was to be alone with Cam. She wondered if Cam realized this.

"Okay," she agreed. "Come on, Jake." Obediently, he walked with her. She held on to his arm, and after a while he seemed to be trembling less.

She had no idea where to take him. But she could see Sleeping Beauty's castle from here, so she headed in that direction. Fantasyland sounded like it would be a lot calmer than Adventureland or Frontierland. As they walked, she spoke softly and gently.

"I'm sorry if this has been too much for you. Humans have experiences they bring to adventures like that, so it's not so disturbing to us. Of course, some of the experiences were new to me, too, but just new enough to make the ride exciting. I guess I forgot that for you, just walking or sitting or holding hands is a whole new experience."

"Yes," he said in that voice that sounded so much like Jake's. If it wasn't so hollow, it would be exactly like Jake's.

"I didn't want to hurt you," she said.

"I realize that," he said. "There is no reason for you to hurt me. There is no reason for any being to hurt any other being."

She wasn't sure if he knew the difference between physical pain and having one's feelings hurt. And did it matter?

"How true." She sighed. "But people don't realize this. Sometimes they want to hurt each other for no reason at all."

They were approaching the castle now, and she pointed it out to him. "It's called the castle of Sleeping Beauty," she told him, "from the old fairy tale, you know."

But of course, he didn't know. Like everything else humans took for granted, fairy tales were mysteries to him.

"Fairy tales are imaginary stories," she explained. "Children like them because they're filled with magic and wonderful adventures. There are princesses and wizards and fairy godmothers. The stories have bad characters in them, too, like witches and ogres and trolls. Sometimes the stories can be pretty scary. But by the end, the good guys always win, and they live happily ever after.''

"This is where these stories happen?'' he asked her.

"Not exactly. I mean, there never really was a Sleeping Beauty or a Snow White or a Cinderella. But this castle is, well, sort of a symbol. It reminds us of when we believed those stories.''

As they crossed the drawbridge and went under the arches, she felt almost magical herself, like she was truly walking into a fairy tale. "When I was a little girl,'' she told him, "this was my favorite fairy tale.''

"What is the story?'' he asked.

She thought back. "I can't remember all the details,'' she confessed. "There was this princess, and when she was born her father, the king, didn't invite some nasty witch to a special ceremony for the baby. But she crashed the party anyway and waited till all the nice witches and sorceresses or whatever they were gave their gifts to the baby.''

"What were the gifts?'' he asked.

"Oh, the usual stuff. Beauty and talent and intelligence—stuff you can only give away in fairy tales. Anyway, to get back at the king, the bad witch made her gift into a curse on the baby princess. She said that when the baby princess turned sixteen she would prick her finger on a poisoned spindle and fall asleep forever.''

"This would be like death?'' he asked.

"Yeah, I guess so.''

"Or like the way I am, the way we all are in my world.''

His words made her want to cry. Quickly, she went back to the story. "But there was still one nice person who hadn't given a gift yet. She couldn't erase the curse, but she added to it. She said that the princess could be woken from her sleep if a prince kissed her." Realizing how dopey this had to sound, she asked, "Does this make any sense at all to you?"

"What is a spindle?" he asked.

"I'm not sure. I think it's something weavers use. Anyway, whatever it is, it has a sharp point. The king got rid of all the spindles in the kingdom so the princess couldn't prick her finger ever."

"And they lived happily ever after," the un-Jake said.

"Oh, no, not yet. Fairy tales are never that easy. You see, that nasty witch planted a spindle in the castle, in some little room no one ever used. One day, when the princess was wandering around, she came into that room and saw this old lady spinning. The old lady was really the witch. She asked the princess if she wanted to try spinning, and the princess did. It was all a trick, of course. The spindle was poisoned, the princess pricked her finger and fell asleep. And so did everyone else in the kingdom."

They were inside the castle now. The un-Jake looked around. "This is where they all fell asleep."

"Not actually," she said. "This story is just make-believe—it's fiction. It's all pretend, not real."

"But this castle is real," he pointed out. "I can touch it."

"Well, yeah, but . . ." She realized it was all too

complicated to explain, and she decided to wind up the story. "Anyway, this prince from far away heard about all this, and he came here and kissed her, everyone woke up, the prince married the princess, and *then* they lived happily ever after."

He nodded. "Was she unconscious for a long time?"

"Oh, yes. Hundreds of years. It had to be pretty strange for her when she woke up. Everything would be different."

"As it is for me," he said.

"Yeah, sort of."

"I am like the princess?"

She looked up at him. For a moment there, he seemed to be wearing the kind of expression she'd seen many times on Jake's face—quizzical, curious, interested. She felt unaccountably warm.

"Well, in your case, the roles would be reversed," she said. "You'd be the prince who was sleeping, and a princess would have to come looking for you and awaken you with a kiss."

He looked at her for what seemed to be a very long time. "I am the prince," he said. "Then you can be the princess."

"I guess I could be the princess," she said. Her voice was barely above a whisper. Was this creature ready for another new experience? Was she ready to provide it?

She put her hands on his shoulders and gazed up at him. Like a knee-jerk reaction, his next movement seemed instinctive. He put his arms around her, bent his head, and kissed her.

Ashley closed her eyes. He felt like Jake, he smelled like Jake, he kissed like Jake. It was right and good and perfectly natural. And what followed the kiss felt absolutely right, too.

When Alex finally located Shalini, he was not in a very good mood.

Where have you been?

Meeting people.

Real people? Humans? Or spooks?

Some humans. And others too. They're not spooky, Alex.

No, they're just creatures from Night of the Living Dead, *that's all. They're turning the humans into blobs, Shalini. They don't even want to fight anymore. They claim they like it here.*

There are aspects of this world that are very likable, Alex.

You can't be serious.

The way they exist together in harmony, equality. There's no cruelty here, nothing to be afraid of.

Ohmigod, they got to you. I knew this would happen if I let you out of my sight. I mean, out of my— my whatever. You've been brainwashed.

I haven't been brainwashed, Alex.

Are you going to tell me you want to stay here?

No, I don't want to stay here. But I want to take something of this place with me back home. I want to invite them to come to Earth.

Shalini, you're nuts. They can't exist on Earth without bodies.

But they can have bodies, Alex. They can share ours.

Now he felt pretty damned sure that somehow or another, Shalini's mind had been utterly destroyed.

nine

kesha knew they were all there, together. Of course, "there" had no meaning here. But she was aware of being able to communicate with seven members of the group. Martha, Donna, Travis, Alex, Shalini, Jake, and David. Ashley and Cam were still on Earth.

A meeting had been called. She didn't know how she knew that, but she knew. One moment she'd been deep in conversation with Corey, talking about movies. They'd debated whether Spike Lee's films could be labeled racist and had just gotten into the question of whether Woody Allen's movies could really be understood by anyone who didn't know New York well.

Suddenly, out of nowhere, she realized that she'd been summoned to a meeting. Without wanting to, she left Corey, and now she was in this meeting. Would she ever become accustomed to this bizarre mode of communication?

She knew who had called the meeting—Jake. Not Travis, who was supposed to be the leader of this expedition. She wondered how Travis felt about this. She soon found out.

Jake began.

I think it would be good for each of us to describe our personal reactions to our experiences here and to share what we've learned about this place. Travis? Do you want to go first?

Jake's voice had penetrated Kesha's consciousness loud and clear. But the response of the usually strong and assertive Travis was barely understandable. When Kesha was able to make out his words, they seemed to be emerging from the mouth of a child.

I want to go home. I can't stand this. I'm not me. I don't know who I am.

Donna quickly took over for him.

This place is terrible, we have to get out of here right away.

Jake wanted to know why Donna thought it was such a terrible place, and Donna had no problem expressing herself.

Are you serious? Look what this place has done to Travis! To all of us! It's awful. We're invisible; we can't see or hear anything; we can't do anything. We're nothing here.

Kesha, who felt more of a something, more of a somebody, than she'd ever felt on Earth, suddenly understood why her best friend would feel this way. Donna's love for Travis colored everything. She couldn't comprehend a world where someone like Travis wouldn't be important, admired, looked up to.

It was Travis who couldn't be anyone here—Travis, whose entire persona was based on his appearance, his style, his attitude. He needed his handsome face, his booming voice. He had to make eye contact if he was going to convince anyone that whatever he said was worth hearing. He was a politician, he was dependent on what people could see in him—no, not *in* him, *on* him. With his facade gone, when all that was important to him had been erased, he was nothing. Or at least, he thought he was nothing. Which pretty much amounted to the same thing.

For the first time ever, Kesha experienced a wave of sympathy for this shallow guy. How strange, she thought, that in this world where no one could actually feel anything, she was feeling more fresh, new emotions than she'd ever experienced before.

Martina was speaking now.

I've been spending all my time with Rosa. Does anyone know how long we've been here, anyway?

No one had the slightest idea. Like everything else that organized and categorized their lives, time had no meaning here. Minutes could have passed since they left Earth—or days or even weeks. For Kesha, the relationship she now had with Corey was the kind of relationship that normally took months to develop.

Martina continued.

Being here with Rosa, it's almost like we were on Earth. Even though we can't see or hear each other, we're the same together. We know each other so well, we understand each other so completely, it doesn't matter where we are or what we're doing. I guess that's why we were able to make that switch so easily back in Central Park. Because we're exactly the same, Rosa and me. In fact, it's like we're really just one person.

But you're not one person. That was David speaking. *I know Rosa in a different way than I know you.*

Martina's response to that came quickly.

David, you're so full of it. Don't you remember the first day of the Disappearance? When we were in the cafeteria at school? You thought I was Rosa; you couldn't tell us apart. You didn't even remember that Rosa wasn't in our geometry class.

David didn't deny that. *But I had a relationship with Rosa. I couldn't have the same relationship with you, Martina.*

Because there's no way in hell I'd ever fall for a creep like you.

But Rosa did. Rosa loved me. Maybe she still does. And you never even liked me; you think I'm slime. So what I'm saying is that you and Rosa aren't the same person.

Even without ears, Kesha could hear the triumph in his voice, and she couldn't blame him for that, because he was making a good point. She was surprised. Who would have thought David could be so astute? If Rosa could feel love for David and Martina could not, then Martina and Rosa had different personalities. They definitely were two different people.

Martina was silent now. She couldn't argue with David, because he was right. Kesha wondered if that idea frightened Martina, knowing that she and her identical twin sister were each distinct, unique, separate, and might someday go their separate ways.

How profound she was becoming, thought Kesha. She never used to have these kinds of insights about people before. Maybe the same insight had come to Martina. Maybe they were all improving, becoming smarter, more sensitive, aware, and just generally *better*.

Her thoughts must have been stronger than she'd intended them to be, because Alex heard her.

Better? You think we're better like this? You've lost your mind—we're all losing our minds. You see what they're doing to us? They're sucking us into their creepy system.

No, Alex, you've got it all wrong.

Kesha was very surprised to realize that this was Shalini who was contradicting Alex so blatantly. And Shalini went on communicating with conviction.

We need them more than they need us. We belong together. Think about Charlotte. She's whole, she's complete, she told us, she's better *now.*

Alex raged. *Shut up, Shalini! Just shut your damned trap. You don't know what you're talking about! No one wants your opinion!* But, to Kesha's mind, Alex now seemed to be more frightened than angry.

Jake took over. *Every opinion is valid, Alex. Even yours.*

Martina wanted to know if Jake knew something that the rest of them didn't know. Jake said yes, he did, and he proceeded to tell them.

They can merge with us. They can enter into us, and live through us. And in a way, everything you say is true, Alex. We will *lose a part of our minds. The part that makes us hate for no reason. The part that prevents us from understanding another point of view. The part that makes us selfish and afraid of getting too close to anyone else. We'll lose our dangerous self-doubts, our meaningless anger, our need to make shallow judgments—*

Alex's thoughts broke in. *And what about independence? We'll lose that too. We're going to all end up like them—one brain, one big fat cosmic communist consciousness.*

That's great alliteration, Alex, but actually we'll be stronger as individuals. Each of us will absorb what we need from the greater spirit. That's all that'll happen—we'll grow. The spirit will fill in the gaps. If you need courage or direction or the ability to love . . . the spirit can help us with that.

Kesha questioned that. *That doesn't make sense, Jake. This spirit, whatever it is, it has no emotion. How can it possibly help us love?*

Because the spirit that binds these beings is the ability to communicate and understand. And if you have these—communication and understanding—you can love.

Kesha wasn't convinced. *But what about the ethics, the morality? This spirit—it kidnapped the human race!*

Because it was the only way it could survive, Kesha.

Now David had a question. *How come you know so much about it? Who have you been conspiring with?*

I'm not conspiring, David, I'm communicating! You remember Jonah. He told me—

Alex broke in again. *Don't tell me you're buying into the garbage that spook is feeding you. You believe this crap?*

Kesha, too, had to question Jonah's credibility.

How do you know he's not lying to you, Jake? Why do you believe him?

Because he's in me now.

Alex had never felt so utterly, totally helpless in his life. It wasn't just the lack of physical form anymore or the inability to fight and defend himself. Something bigger was going on, something more frightening. He was seeing a future that was beyond his imagination.

It was like a movie, one of those spectacular wide-screen films, the kind that gave you the sense of being surrounded. Maybe that was why it was so frightening. This future, it was all around him—he was trapped. He couldn't turn away.

Only, it wasn't *his* future. That wasn't him up on the giant screen. Shalini was in this movie. Yes, that was definitely Shalini up there. He could recognize her even though she was older, in her thirties or forties maybe. She'd left adolescence long behind.

She didn't look all that different, though. Her glossy, straight dark hair was still pulled back tightly away from her face. She had the same huge liquid-brown eyes, the same strong nose, the same red lips. She wasn't wearing her usual long skirt and sweater, though, or the traditional sari she used to wear occasionally at school. She had some kind of uniform on.

It didn't seem to be any kind of military uniform. She wasn't dressed as a police officer either. But, of course, that could never happen. His sweet, naive Shalini with a gun in her hand? No way.

But this was definitely a uniform, some sort of

a jumpsuit, and now he could make out an insignia on the shoulder. NASA. He'd seen that before. What did it stand for? Then he realized she was leading four others, dressed identically, and they were all moving toward some monolith, silver, it looked like an amusement park ride, only bigger. . . .

It was a rocket. This was Cape Canaveral, Florida. Crowds were cheering, a band was playing. Shalini, his sweet, dependent, afraid-of-her-own-shadow Shalini was an astronaut!

Like a scene on the TV news, a scene he'd witnessed times before, the event continued. Shalini and her colleagues entered this—this *thing*, and he could see inside, where they strapped themselves into seats. Shalini was adjusting equipment, barking out orders he couldn't even understand.

Now he was on the outside again. There was a sound like an explosion, orange streaks, smoke. . . . The huge hunk of metal was rising. . . .

And Shalini was in that thing, blasting off into the unknown.

Well, why not? She'd always wanted adventure. She had told him that, way back when they found the circle of flattened grass on the Great Lawn in Central Park. She'd been sheltered and protected and babied all her life, and she'd expressed to him a deep longing to explore and experience. But she never would—he knew that for sure and so did she. She wouldn't leave home, she could never be that strong and independent, it wasn't in her nature. This wasn't her future he was seeing now, it was her fantasy.

It doesn't have to be a fantasy, Alex. I can be that person.

Shalini? Are you there?

But there was no answer. She wasn't there; he was only imagining what she would say to him right now. What she wanted to say, what she wanted him to know. What he couldn't bear to hear.

He thought back to the first time he saw Shalini, really looked at her. It wasn't in the geometry class they'd shared at Madison High before the Disappearance. He'd never looked at anyone in that class—or in the whole school for that matter. They never looked at him either. He was just as invisible at Madison High, Greenwich Village, New York, USA, as he was right here in the middle of nowhere. They had no more interest in knowing him than he had in knowing them. He couldn't say whose lack of interest came first, but what did it matter?

In any case, the first time he really saw Shalini was in a movie theater in SoHo, days after the Disappearance. He'd gone there to set up a movie and watch it by himself. He'd been annoyed when he realized he wasn't alone in the theater.

He'd heard her before he saw her. She was crouched in a seat in the back of the darkened theater, and she was crying. His first impulse was to ignore her, to not become involved. But for some insane reason, he spoke to her, he even asked her what was wrong.

There was nothing unusual happening to her; she was going through what everyone was trying to deal with. Nobody had been too thrilled about coming out of a classroom to find that the rest of the world had disappeared.

But Shalini was even more scared than the rest of them. What was more significant was the fact that she wanted to share her fear with him. She had no friends in that class, no one who could comfort her or help her to feel less alone. Most of the other twenty-five were reacting to the Disappearance with nonstop partying, or at least that's how it seemed at the time. With Shalini's sheltered background, her lack of experience in the world, she needed someone who could be more than a friend.

He remembered how that made him feel, the fact that she was confiding in him. He felt strong, important. He felt like his existence had some meaning.

Shalini needed him. Okay, maybe not him, Alex Popov, but someone like him. Someone who could take care of her, who could protect her, who could ensure that no one would hurt her. And he could do that. As long as he was with her no one would dare threaten her.

No one human, that is. He couldn't fight what threatened her here. What did it matter anyway? If the vision he saw was a true future for Shalini, she didn't need him anymore anyway.

I still need you, Alex.

That was what he wanted to hear. It was a moment before he realized that this was a real communication.

For what? You're going to let this spirit merge with you. You'll be strong and independent and you won't be afraid of everything. You won't need me to protect you anymore.

I don't want your protection, Alex. I want your love.

It occurred to him that they'd never used that word. He'd come to think of Shalini as his girlfriend—it was unspoken, but understood.

He liked the sound of it, or whatever he could call the way he heard her. But it didn't make him feel any better.

Did you see that movie, Shalini? You're going to be an astronaut. That's your future. I don't have a future. Twenty years from now, I'll be a small-time hood back in Brooklyn—if there is a Brooklyn. I'll be in jail. Or I'll be a junkie. Or I'll be dead.

But that's not how it has to be, Alex. You're smart. You're full of anger, but that's not a bad thing. If you could channel that anger, direct it, you could do something wonderful in the world.

That's not me. I can't do that.

He expected—he hoped—she would argue that with him. She didn't. She actually agreed with him.

Not now, Alex. You can't do that now; you don't have it in you now. But you could.

Charlotte wasn't shocked when Ashley attempted to tell her what happened between her and the un-Jake in Sleeping Beauty's castle. Ashley couldn't quite come right out and say it—she hinted and implied. But there was no way Charlotte couldn't figure out what Ashley was really saying. And she didn't scold her or judge her or even look embarrassed.

"You made love."

"Yes."

They were back at the farm now. Cam had gone

off to check on the other aliens. The un-Jake had gone into the labyrinth. That was Charlotte's suggestion. He wasn't shaking anymore, but he wasn't speaking either.

Ashley could see him now, standing in the center of the spiral path, not moving. She wondered what was going on in his head, what sort of memory he retained of the experience they'd shared less than an hour earlier.

"It wasn't just sex," she told Charlotte. "I mean, I'm not trying to make it sound mystical and magical, but it had a meaning."

"I believe that," Charlotte said.

"It felt right. He needed this. He needed *me*."

"Did you need him?" Charlotte asked.

"I needed Jake," Ashley confessed. "I looked at him, and I saw Jake."

"That makes sense," Charlotte agreed.

"But he's *not* Jake! And now I feel so—so—"

"What?"

"Wrong. Guilty. Like I betrayed Jake. Like I cheated on him behind his back."

"But you didn't," Charlotte pointed out. "You *were* with Jake. He just wasn't all there."

Ashley was silent for a moment. "It *felt* like I was with Jake," she confessed. "And it was nice. It didn't feel wrong, not while it was happening. Maybe that's why I feel so awful now."

Charlotte burst out laughing. "Are you saying you'd feel better if you hadn't enjoyed it?"

Ashley blushed. "Yeah, maybe. Hell, I don't know how I feel. And what's Jake going to think? Will he know that I did this? Oh, let's not talk about it, it's too complicated. Making love with your boyfriend's body when his mind is who knows where. Making *normal* love is complicated enough, y'know?''

"No."

"Huh?"

"No, I don't know," Charlotte said. "I've never made love before."

"Oh. That's cool—you just haven't met the right person yet."

Charlotte sighed. "I'm not sure if that's it. I mean, I used to think I couldn't meet the right person, because I wasn't open to it, you know? I was afraid to get that close to another person." She smiled. "But I'm not afraid anymore. That's what the spirit did for me, Ashley. Remember, before you came, I was alone here, and the spirit was within me. I had to get to know myself, and the spirit helped me to break through the barriers that prevent us from knowing ourselves. The fear, the need to protect ourselves—it got me through that." She was still smiling, but her eyes were serious. "The spirit doesn't bring miracles, Ashley. I can still get hurt, I can still have my heart broken, but I'm willing to take the chance."

"So all you have to do now is wait for Mr. Right to come along," Ashley said.

"I think he already has." Charlotte was looking past Ashley, in the direction of the swimming pool.

"Cam?"

"Mm. I think he's very special."

Ashley was pleased. "That's great!"

Charlotte shook her head. "But *he's* not ready. He's never given much credit to emotions, Ashley. Maybe he's afraid, too. It's like there's a part of him that's missing—or buried or something. He won't let me get really close.''

''That can change,'' Ashley said.

Charlotte nodded. ''Maybe. If he *wants* it.'' She turned and looked back out at the labyrinth. ''Jake's coming back,'' she noted.

''The un-Jake,'' Ashley corrected her. But as the figure on the circular path drew closer, she felt her heart skip a beat.

Charlotte was right. It was Jake.

ten

ashley watched as the figure of Jake approached. He was taking his time as he rounded the curves of the labyrinth. He had his hands in his pockets, and his head was bowed, as if he were thinking very hard about something. She resisted an impulse to run to him.

Charlotte had tactfully taken off, so by the time Jake emerged from the labyrinth Ashley was alone to greet him. Now that she could really see his face, she experienced a moment of uncertainty.

"Jake? Is that you?"

"It's me," he said, and he smiled.

Still, she didn't dash forward to embrace him, and he didn't make any frantic rush to her either. She wondered if he could be feeling suddenly, oddly, shy—the way she was feeling at the moment.

"How are you?" she asked. It seemed like a pretty lame thing to say, under the circumstances.

"I'm okay," he replied. "Anyone else back yet?"

Ashley looked in the direction of the swimming pool, which was the last place she'd seen them all gathered. "I don't think so. No one's gone into the labyrinth."

"They may not need to," Jake told her.

"Why, what happened? What was it like there? Did you see Corey?" She stopped, not wanting to bombard him with questions after what must have been a pretty arduous journey. But Jake didn't seem overwhelmed.

"Let's go somewhere," he said. "Away from here."

"Where?" She hoped he wasn't about to suggest Disneyland.

"Anywhere."

"Okay."

Charlotte had told them that the Jeep was at their disposal, whenever they wanted to use it. As they got into the car, it occurred to her that only a couple of hours had passed since she'd been in the Jeep with the other—with the un-Jake. A wave of guilt washed over her. She glanced furtively at Jake.

Was it at all possible that he knew what had happened between her and the other one? Did he have any memory of what his body had done on Earth?

Surely not. She knew her Jake. She knew she'd sense the hurt and anger he'd be feeling. There was no way he'd be able to keep up this calm demeanor in the face of her stupid behavior. So now there remained the big question—would she tell him?

Jake had figured out how to start the Jeep. He shifted gears, backed out, and began to head across the field.

"Where are we going?" Ashley asked.

"I don't know," Jake replied. "Where do you want to go?"

She considered this. It had to be a place where she felt relaxed and tranquil, a place with the right atmosphere. Because she realized now that there was no way she would be able to keep this a secret from him. She was going to tell him what happened, and she needed all the emotional strength she could gather. "Do you think we could find the ocean?"

"It's pretty big," Jake said. "If we head in the right direction, I don't see how we can miss it." It was the kind of dumb joke he was always making, and she didn't know whether to be relieved or frightened. The old Jake would never be able to forgive her.

As a native New Yorker, Jake wasn't quite as confident as Charlotte had been behind the wheel of the Jeep. But fortunately there were no other moving vehicles that could suffer as a result of his inexperience. He managed to get them moving in a westward direction, toward the Pacific.

As he drove, he told Ashley about his experience. She listened to his matter-of-fact description of life without form, how it felt to communicate telepathically. He told her what he had learned about the entity that controlled their fate, why the people on Earth had been taken away, and why their little group had been left behind.

It was like hearing the plot of a very far-fetched, bad science fiction movie. And yet at the same time it was all completely logical; it all made sense. The questions they'd been asking themselves since the

Disappearance were now answered. The pieces of the puzzle were falling into place.

"So what happens now?" she asked him. "Will they let everyone return?"

"I'm not sure," he said. "I *think* so. But there's a catch."

"What's the catch?"

"They want to come with us."

"How?"

"In us, all of us. In everyone on the face of the Earth."

She listened in a daze as he explained the prospect of merging. The magnitude of what he was proposing took her breath away. Suddenly, all she could think of was the *Exorcist*, or the *Alien* movie series. Something alive, inside of her, breathing, growing . . . "Jake, stop the car!"

He did. She jumped out, ran a few steps, and doubled over. She thought she would throw up, but nothing happened. The nausea passed.

Jake was just behind her, and his strong, comforting hands held her. "No, it wouldn't be like that."

She turned sharply. "Can you read my mind?"

He grinned. "No, that telepathy stuff doesn't work here. I'm just making a pretty good guess at what you're thinking. That we'd all be possessed— or something like that."

"They're more powerful than we are, Jake! Look at what they were able to do. If they're in us, they'll take us over!"

He shook his head. "But that's not what it's all about. Look at Charlotte! She's got the spirit in her. Does she seem possessed to you?"

"We don't know what she was like before," Ashley pointed out to him.

"I'll bet she was exactly the way she is now," Jake said. "Just—less."

"What does *that* mean?"

"I think she was incomplete. Like all of us, our personalities are fractured. There's a piece missing. We're not what we can be. We're not what we're supposed to be."

Ashley frowned. "You're not going to start talking psychobabble to me, are you?" They returned to the car and took off. Ashley rolled down the window and took a deep breath. She could smell the salt water now.

"We're getting close," she told him. And now the ocean was visible, just at the horizon. She could see turquoise water flecked with foam. As they drove closer, she could make out the rolling waves, moving in steady rhythms, lapping at the shore.

As if by unspoken agreement, they didn't speak again until they had driven onto the beach and gotten out of the Jeep. Ashley took off her sandals and started to walk barefoot on the warm sand. But Jake suddenly clutched her arms and forced her to face him.

"Ashley, I think they belong in us. They're supposed to be part of us. Maybe they were part of us—or something like them was—back in the beginning of time. It's the part of us that keeps us connected, that keeps us involved with all other living things. But something happened. Somehow, as we evolved, we lost that instinctive ability to care. We stressed independence and became totally self-absorbed, self-serving. We couldn't perceive beyond ourselves; we weren't able to believe that any one else's existence could be as important as our own. That's the part of us that's missing. If we merge, we'll have that part of us back. It's right, it's good.''

"But how can you know that for sure?" Ashley wanted to know. Then, she knew. He didn't have to answer her. She could see it in his eyes. "You've merged."

"Yes. And, Ashley, I'm the same person I always was. I'm just better."

"Better *how*?" she cried out.

"Lots of ways."

"Give me one concrete example," she demanded.

He thought. "Okay, here's something. Remember back when we were in the Community, and I was always telling you how beautiful you were? And you'd get angry at me for thinking about your looks all the time?"

Ashley remembered this well, but she didn't recall ever actually telling him how she felt about it. "You knew I was angry at you?"

"I didn't then. I do now. And I understand why it would make you angry. Maybe I would have figured that out eventually. But you would have been long gone." She couldn't argue with that. She remembered how quickly she'd left him back at the health club. "You see the difference, Ashley? I can truly care about you now, and not just in relation to me. I don't need a trophy girlfriend, I need *you*. I love *you*, for everything you are. The real you, not the supermodel. I'm beyond all that now. We can all get past that, if we can really care."

She felt an urge to kiss him, or at least take his hand. But she was afraid to touch him until she had the answer to another question.

"Jake, now that you've merged . . . do you know what your body did, here on Earth, while you were gone? What we called the un-Jake—do you have his memories?"

"Yes."

She felt a sickening thud in the pit of her stomach. At the same time, she was relieved. She wouldn't have been able to keep it a secret from him. "What do you know?"

"We went to Disneyland. We rode on the Astro Orbiter. We made love."

She couldn't look at him. She pulled away and faced in the direction of the sea. "I'm sorry. I don't know what else to say. It was a terrible thing to do, I don't know why I did it, maybe I was just lonely, but it felt right—"

He broke in. "You don't have to explain, and you don't have to apologize."

Now *that* was a little too much. No one could be that open-minded. She whirled around. "But you must be angry! You have to feel betrayed—or jealous or something! Either you're mad about what I did, or mad that I didn't tell you right away—"

"But you didn't betray me! Ashley, we made love. *We* made love! That's what I'm trying to tell you. That spirit, that entity, the un-Jake, whatever you want to call it, he was part of me. That's why I don't feel betrayed. How could I possibly be jealous of myself?"

She gazed at him in wonderment. There was a

strange kind of logic to what he was saying, but she still wasn't ready to buy it.

"Think about it," he persisted. "You just said it yourself: it felt right. Why did it feel right? Could you have made love with a total stranger and felt that way about it?"

"No, of course not. But that doesn't make it right. He looked like you, but he wasn't you."

"He was a part of me," Jake stated. "Ashley, if he wasn't a part of me, don't you think I'd be pretty pissed off right now?"

Now Ashley could see a flaw in his logic. "But you can't get pissed off," she declared triumphantly. "You said so yourself, remember? The new you can't be angry at me because you love me so completely!"

"Not true," Jake said, and hastily amended that. "I mean, it's true that I love you completely. But if there's a real reason to get angry, something that isn't just a blow to my ego, believe me, I can still get angry."

He looked so earnest she had to believe him. And then she was able to touch him.

They held each other, clinging to each other, but not out of any sense of desperation or fear. At least, *she* didn't feel anything but pure, unadulterated joy. She knew she was with her Jake, the real Jake, possessed by nothing more than a love for her.

Hand in hand, they walked along in comfortable silence for a while, staying close to the water so the tide could lick their feet.

"Will everyone merge?" she asked him finally. "This spirit, can it make everyone accept it?"

"No. We have to want it. We have to be open to it."

"So what's the process? Do we go into the labyrinth? I can't believe that every person on Earth is going to do that."

"No, that's not how it works. I've got this feeling that the whole Earth has become the center of a cosmic labyrinth. If you're willing to accept the spirit, it'll just happen."

After a moment, she asked him, "How will I know when it's happened?"

"You'll know."

And she did. No bolt of lightening shot through her, she didn't feel an electrical charge or some overwhelming sense of well-being. But by the time they returned to the farm, she knew she was whole, and complete.

She wasn't the only one.

Travis and Donna were the first ones they saw. They were sitting at the kitchen table, and Travis looked distinctly uncomfortable.

"His pants are too tight," Donna explained. "He must have really pigged out. I mean, the part of him that was here."

"I'm going to have to watch that from now on," Travis said worriedly.

Ashley understood what he meant. Before, Travis never did anything to extremes. He kept a tight rein on all his feelings, his instincts, his desires. His concern for his image, for the way he looked and the way others saw him, would always keep him from overeating.

Now he wasn't in total control of himself anymore, not the way he used to be. That false self-confidence, the sense of superiority, all that was gone now. He'd have to be honest now, to deal with the person he really was, whoever that might be. Ashley wondered if Donna would be able to love a Travis who wasn't the master of the universe.

But at this moment, Donna didn't seem at all perturbed by Travis's newfound sense of insecurity. Ashley realized that Donna, too, had to have become a more fully evolved person. Now she was the kind of girl who wouldn't be so easily seduced by shallow charisma.

They left Travis longingly eyeing a bag of cookies, and went outside. They could see Alex and Shalini sitting on a bench. They appeared to be having an intense conversation. Ashley smiled. That was another couple who would have to rethink their relationship. If the missing elements in their personalities had been recovered, Shalini would no longer be willing to let Alex dominate her so completely. But on the other hand, Alex wouldn't have the need to be so domineering.

And what about David Chu? Somehow, Ashley couldn't believe that any infusion of ethics would curb his need to conquer every woman on the face of the Earth. But maybe now, he'd care about what happened to them.

With Jake, she walked across the grass toward the orchard. She didn't feel any need to fill up the quiet with chatter, the way she used to. Was this one of the ways that she had changed? Funny, how much easier it was to determine how others had changed, but it was hard to identify the changes in yourself. But in a way, that made perfect sense. She wasn't so obsessed with herself anymore. What was happening to other people meant just as much to her.

"Look at that," Jake said suddenly.

It was Cam and Charlotte, under a tree, embracing passionately. Ashley was so happy for Charlotte.

And then she realized another change in herself—the ability to be happy for someone else. No, more than that—she couldn't only see Charlotte's happiness, the happiness made *her* feel happy, as happy as she'd be if something that lovely was happening to her.

But maybe that wasn't the best analogy, she thought, as she felt Jake slip his arm around her shoulders. Because something that lovely *was* happening to her.

eleven

"**can you remember** what to do?'' Donna asked Travis. "Do you still know how to fly a plane?''

He replied with some irritation. "Of course I still know how to fly a plane. I was flying a plane the day before yesterday, remember? I'm not going to forget how to fly in forty-eight hours.''

Donna spoke patiently. "But you're not the same person you were the day before yesterday, Travis. You're not so sure of yourself anymore.''

"Don't remind me,'' he muttered.

"So I'm just checking, to make sure that you still feel confident about flying, that's all.''

"Don't worry about it, I'm fine,'' he said a little testily. But there were little lines of concern on his forehead that hadn't been there forty-eight hours ago.

"It's kind of hard to take in,'' Kesha mused out loud. "We only arrived here two days ago. It feels like we've been here for ages.''

Alex had to admit it was all pretty strange. "I'll be glad when time starts to feel like something normal.''

He'd be glad when *he* started to feel normal. But

at this point in whatever time it was, he couldn't be sure what normal would feel like. Or if he'd ever felt normal before. Maybe the way he felt right now was going to be normal from now on. If that was the case, it wasn't so bad.

They were all together at the Los Angeles airport. Charlotte had brought them out there in the bus. Cam was still trying to talk her into going back to New York with them.

"I can't, Cam. Not now. I have to be here when everyone comes back. I'm sure my parents are going to be in a pretty freaky state of mind. The last thing they need is to find me missing."

"I could stay," Cam began, but then he shook his head. "No, I've got parents, too.

"You really think they're all coming back?" Kesha asked.

Jake answered. "Everyone's coming back. We need to get things ready for them. Charlotte's right, Cam. Everything's got to be as normal as possible."

"We'll talk on the phone," Charlotte promised him. "And as soon as we can, we'll be together."

Alex marveled at the way Mr. Techno-Dork was reacting to this separation. The poor jerk was positively heartbroken—there was tragedy written all over his pale, freckled face.

He could sympathize, though. If Shalini and he were ever separated from each other . . .

Where *was* Shalini? He looked around and spotted her over by the tail of the plane with David and Ashley. Chu was leaning against the plane with his arms crossed, and he was giving both Shalini and Ashley his I'm-so-gorgeous-and-sexy-you-can't-resist-me look. Of course, Shalini wasn't buying it. That was one thing Alex would never have to worry about—losing Shalini to a lamebrain lady-killer like David Chu. She had better taste.

They were ready to go back to New York. Jake thought it was best that they all try to be where they were when the rest of the world vanished.

Martina had been dismayed by the suggestion, and she was still making this known. "I hope we're not going to have to sit in geometry class and wait for everyone to come back."

"We don't have to go back to Madison," Jake assured her. "But I think we should be in the general vicinity."

"I wonder what the rest of the Community has been doing," Donna asked no one in particular.

Martina had an answer. "They've been having an endless party. That's all they ever wanted. They're dancing in the streets—they've probably turned Manhattan into one gigantic dance club."

Kesha agreed. "I can see them now. They're all drunk—or stoned—and they haven't bathed since we left."

Shalini joined them and caught Kesha's words. "I don't think it's going to be that bad. I can't imagine Maura going two days without washing her hair."

But Travis radiated gloom. "It's going to be an anarchy, I know it. No order, no organization. They've all turned into animals. Remember *Lord of the Flies*?"

Donna patted his arm. "You'll straighten them out."

"How?" Travis asked helplessly. "They're not going to listen to me."

Alex thought how weird it was, watching the know-it-all big shot act so insecure. To be perfectly honest, he liked the pompous ass better this way.

"Let's get going," Jake said.

Cam and Charlotte went into a farewell that was almost embarrassing to watch. Alex helped David to drag a movable staircase to the door of the plane so they could get in.

"Hold this," David said, thrusting a large bag at Travis.

Travis obliged. "What's in it?"

"Stuff to eat. Candy bars, Twinkies. Dried beef jerky."

Jake frowned. "Damn, I didn't think about food."

"There's plenty for everyone," David assured him. They all climbed into the plane.

Travis was still fretful. "You don't think everyone's going to start coming back while we're in the air, do you? Maybe I should file a flight pattern, just in case. I don't want to be bouncing around up there when the 747s start taking off again."

Jake looked pained. "Travis, folks are coming back to Earth, they're getting into their bodies, they're going to need some time to adjust. I don't think anyone's going to be booking their vacation flights any time soon."

"But there were planes in the air at the time of the Disappearance," Travis said persistently.

"And there were cars on the roads," Jake reminded him. "But the spirit is aware, Travis. They're not going to put us in danger." He grinned. "Our bodies are too valuable."

"Jake's right," Donna said to Travis. "Just calm down, okay? We'll play it by ear."

Shalini whispered into Alex's ear. "I think she likes being in charge for a change."

Alex looked at her with more than a little anxiety. Did Shalini think *she* was going to start ordering *him* around now? Actually, he couldn't blame her if she tried. As she strode on ahead of him up the stairs, he wondered how she'd ever put up with the way he used to push her around. For the life of him, he couldn't understand what had made him behave so aggressively.

They were all on the plane now. Cam's face was glued to a window, and as he stared through the glass at Charlotte, Alex could swear Mr. Science was crying. Donna was in the cockpit with Travis, still bolstering him with encouraging words. David was passing around his bag of munchies. When the bag reached Alex, he poked around inside and pulled out two Snickers bars, his favorite candy. He handed one to Shalini.

She handed it back to him. "I don't like caramel."

He was surprised. She used to eat the Snickers he gave her without question. "You never told me that," he said.

"You never asked me what I liked," Shalini replied. "I'm telling you now."

The engines began to roar, the plane shuddered, and then it started down the runway. Alex got a sick feeling in the pit of his stomach. "I don't like to fly," he confessed to Shalini.

"You never told me that before," Shalini said.

He smiled thinly. "I'm telling you now."

Shalini took his hand. "I'm here," she said comfortingly.

Funny, how he never before realized that he might need her as much as she needed him.

Kesha woke to the sound of Travis's voice over the intercom.

"We're starting the descent now. We should be on the ground in fifteen minutes."

There was no response in the cabin. At first, Kesha thought everyone else was sleeping. Then she realized they were all just being very quiet. Faces were pressed against the windows.

At the moment, they were still in the clouds. Kesha tried to remember what it used to look like when she'd looked out of the window of a landing plane. The clouds would separate into wisps of cotton, and land would appear like a patchwork quilt. Then you'd make out the lines dividing the land, then the bigger buildings, and the lines became roads, with tiny ants moving along them. Then the ants became cars and trucks . . . sometimes you saw more. Once, Kesha had flown on the evening of the fourth of July, and she'd seen fireworks. That had been amazing.

But as they sank below the clouds, there was nothing like that to be seen. No fireworks, and no ants either. If anyone had expected to see any dramatic change on Earth, they'd be disappointed. There were no more signs of life now than there had been the day they landed in Los Angeles.

Jake broke the silence with an observation. "The

air looks cleaner now. I can see more than I used to.''

"That makes sense,'' David said. "It's been over two months without any exhaust from cars and trucks. No cigarette smoke, no factories pumping poisonous fumes in the atmosphere, no garbage burning. The environment is probably cleaner now than any time since the Industrial Revolution. I wonder if there's any way we can keep it like this.''

"Since when did you get so interested in protecting the environment?'' Martina asked him.

"I don't know,'' David said, and he sounded truly puzzled.

But Kesha knew. It was the spirit they had merged with. It was making them all care, in some way or another. When you stopped thinking of yourself as an isolated entity, you started to see the world differently. You realized how all aspects of everything affected everyone.

She wondered how it would affect the rest of humanity. No, that was too overwhelming to consider. She settled on thinking about her own family and the changes she might expect to see in them. Her grandmother, for example, the great worrier, the one who claimed she carried the weight of the world on her shoulders. She'd always cared about everything and everyone. Would she be the same, or more so? Kesha couldn't envision her grandmother being any kinder or warmer than she already was.

And what about her oldest brother, Ken? His chief characteristic had always been his cynicism, his bitterness, his lack of belief or trust in anyone, particularly white people. Somehow, she couldn't imagine Ken suddenly loving all of humanity. That wouldn't be him.

And how would *she* change? Or had she changed already, and hadn't realized it?

There was a whooshing sound, a bump, then another bump. The plane had landed at John F. Kennedy Airport, where Travis was able to sail along rapidly on an empty runway to the terminal building. It was just as deserted as it had been when they'd taken off.

Everyone got busy, and there was no time to think. They split into groups, climbed into cars, and started back to Manhattan. Nothing had changed— the expressway was still clogged with vehicles, and they had to abandon their cars every few minutes and switch to others. Kesha was driving one car, with Cam and Martina as passengers.

Martina was in the front passenger seat, looking out the window. "I thought it might be different by now."

"How different?" Kesha asked her.

"I guess I thought everything would be like it was, before the Disappearance. Everyone would be back on Earth."

"It'll happen," Kesha said. "We're talking about billions of people, remember? They're not going to return like *that*." She removed her hand from the wheel long enough to snap her fingers.

"I don't see why not," Martina said. "They disappeared just like that."

"Yeah, but now they have to merge with the spirit," Kesha pointed out. "That could take a while, I guess."

"They got us merged and back on Earth fast enough," Martina said.

"But are we merged?" Kesha wondered out loud. "Do you think you've changed? Do you feel different?"

Martina was silent for a minute. "I can see how some of the others have changed," she said finally. "I mean, think about Shalini. She was actually expressing opinions back there on the plane."

"But what about you?" Kesha persisted.

"I can't tell."

"Neither can I. Cam?"

Her passenger in the backseat hadn't spoken for a while. "Huh?"

"What do you think?"

"About what?"

"He's thinking about Charlotte," Martina said. "We can all see what the merger's done for you, Cam."

"What do you mean?"

"Well, you never had a girlfriend before, right?"

"Maybe I just never met the right girl before," Cam said.

"Nah, I think getting the spirit makes you capable of loving someone," Martina told him.

"There is absolutely no scientific evidence to substantiate that," Cam declared. "Besides, how do you know this whole thing hasn't been a dream?"

"What are you saying?" Kesha asked. "We all fell asleep in geometry and we're going to wake up back in the bomb shelter at Madison?"

"It's possible," Cam said.

"No way," Kesha declared. "I always know when I'm dreaming."

"We could be hallucinating," Cam suggested. "You know, that bomb shelter gets very little fresh air. Carbon monoxide could have formed. It could have reached a level where we were all knocked into a coma. We could be having some sort of massive shared hallucination."

Martina laughed uneasily. "You make this sound like an episode of *The X-Files*."

They'd reached the 59th Street Bridge, which was completely clogged with cars and trucks and totally impassable. They got out of the car and started across on foot.

"Did you see the episode where Scully was abducted?" Cam continued. "We still don't know if that really happened or not."

"You're talking about a TV show," Kesha said. "*The X-Files* is science fiction. This is real, Cam."

"Reality is subjective," Cam intoned. "Okay, maybe it wasn't a hallucination. But we've been in California. Our perceptions of reality could have been completely altered."

"Oh, shut up," Martina said good-naturedly. They'd reached the end of the bridge, where they found a van that wasn't blocked. "Kesha, can you drive a stick shift?"

She could, but not very well. They entered the borough of Manhattan in fits and starts as she attempted to shift gears. After being tossed around inside the van for several blocks, they decided to continue downtown on foot at the blocked intersection of 42nd Street and Broadway.

If the members of the Community who had been

left behind had gone on any kind of a wild and drunken rampage, it wasn't evident here. Times Square was Times Square, its modern, gleaming glass and metal structures keeping uneasy company with the seedy remnants of its past. Posters advertising elaborate Broadway musicals still shared space with signs luring nonexistent tourists into pornographic movie theaters.

"You know, I've never been to a real Broadway show," Martina said suddenly. "I've never been to Radio City Music Hall either."

"What does that have to do with anything?" Kesha asked.

"Nothing. I guess."

But Kesha had a feeling she knew why Martina's thoughts were turning in this direction. There were lots of experiences they hadn't had. And they were all hoping they'd have another chance to experience them.

"Have you ever been to the Macy's Thanksgiving Day parade?" Shalini asked Alex as they crossed 34th Street.

"No," Alex said.

"Me neither. Do you realize that Thanksgiving is only two weeks from now?"

Alex thought about that. "I don't think we should expect a real parade this year," he said.

"Maybe not," she said. "But the next time there's a Thanksgiving Day parade, let's go, okay?"

It wasn't an activity that had ever appealed to Alex before, but he thought he could bear it. "Okay."

They'd driven from the airport with Ashley and Jake. Along the way, they'd spotted Travis, Donna, and David walking, and now they were all walking down Fifth Avenue together. By the time they reached 23rd Street, everyone's pace was slowing down, and Alex didn't think this was because they were particularly tired. It was just that no one was in a rush to get back to the hotel in SoHo. They had no idea what they'd find there.

Would that ape, Mike Salicki, be guarding the door with a machine gun? Who would be running the show—an idiot like Scott Spivey?

"I'm hungry," Ashley announced suddenly.

Everyone latched onto that as an excuse to take a break, and they went into the closest restaurant. There, in a back room, Jake discovered a huge freezer which held frozen beef patties, buns, and slices of processed American cheese. He pried them apart and formed frozen sandwiches that he stuck into the microwave.

Alex found an unopened jar of Thousand Island dressing. "Do you think that stuff is safe to eat?" Donna asked.

Alex read the label. "There's enough preservative in here to keep it edible till the next millennium." He unscrewed the lid, and it emitted a reassuring pop.

The dressing gave the burgers something that resembled a taste. "These are almost like Big Macs," Ashley said happily as she started on her second sandwich. "You know what, guys? I'm going to miss being able to eat like this. When I start modeling again I'll have to go back to living on lettuce and carrot sticks." She rubbed her nearly bald head. "I'll have to let my hair grow back too. Just when I'm getting used to this."

"I could never be a model," Donna stated. "Life's too short to starve yourself. People should be able to eat anything they want."

"And as much as they want," Travis echoed. He was on his third burger. It was clear to Alex that the spirit was allowing Travis to indulge himself.

"I wonder why models have to be skinny anyway," Ashley mused. "It's not like being thin automatically means being beautiful."

David looked at her. "Yeah, that's what I think. Personally, I like a girl with some meat on her."

Ashley gave him a withering look, but David just grinned. Alex was mildly relieved to see that David hadn't changed completely.

When they were all satisfied, there was no excuse to put off the journey any longer. The seven of them continued down the avenue. It was when they reached Eighth Street that they all became aware of an odd, unfamiliar noise. It was a rumbling sound, and it was coming from the direction of Washington Square.

"What is that?" Travis asked.

"It sounds like machinery," Shalini said. Their pace quickened, and they all started walking in that direction. The noise became louder, and they started to run. Alex was just behind Travis, who was taller than he was. He tried to move around Travis to get a better view but crashed right into him.

"Watch it!" Travis yelled.

"Aw, shut up and move," Alex retorted. As the

words left his mouth, he was relieved to know that he, too, had retained elements of his disposition.

But all thoughts of personality flew out of his mind as he took in the view of Washington Square Park. Smack in the center of the grassy lawn stood a bulldozer, the kind you usually saw around a construction site.

"What the hell is that doing here?" Jake exclaimed.

They were all frozen by the sight. As they watched, the big mouthlike thing cut into the earth and lifted out a huge chunk, leaving behind a gouge in the land.

"Can you see who's running it?" Alex asked Jake.

"It looks like Carlos Guzman," Jake said. "Has he lost his mind?"

They watched him dump the dirt into a growing pile, and then dig into the park for another chunk. In a state of shock, they reached the edge of the park and took in the whole scene.

Carlos wasn't alone in the park. Members of the Community were spread out all over the grassy expanse, and most of them seemed to be chopping the earth or digging with shovels.

"Hey!" Jake yelled. "What are you doing?"

But the noise of the bulldozer drowned out his voice. Several people noticed them standing on the edge of the park, and a couple of people waved, but they went right on digging. Scott, Mike, and Kyle were digging just nearby, and they glanced at the group. No one seemed surprised to see them. No one asked where they'd been. Alex got the feeling they knew.

"What's going on?" Jake asked.

"We're going to bury rotten food here," Mike told him.

Jake was aghast. "You're turning Washington Square into a landfill?"

"It's organic stuff," Mike told him. "It's okay. So grab a shovel and get to work or shut your mouth."

"Where did you get the bulldozer?" Travis wanted to know.

"There was some construction going on over by the Hudson," Scott said. "We figured out a path, and moved the cars into a high-rise garage. It wasn't easy, let me tell you. We could have used some more help. I think I moved about a thousand cars myself."

"Bull," Mike said succinctly. "You didn't do half that. And I'll tell you something else. People aren't going to be too thrilled when they come back to Earth and can't find their cars."

"Too bad," Scott said. "What was I supposed to do, keep a list of where every car went? You think I'm a car hop?"

"I guess their cars won't be the first things on their minds," Jake said.

"No kidding," Kyle said. "What about all those guys who haven't had sex for two months?"

Mike sneered. "Like you've been on a roll? Cut the crap, Bailey."

Kyle grinned. "I've done okay. There's more than one happy girl on this Earth right now."

Alex tried to make some sense out of what he was hearing. Scott was still whining, just like Alex remembered him doing back when they were in the

Community. Mike was still a bully and Kyle was still a sexist pig. So what did this mean? What had the merger accomplished?

But Jake's eyes were shining. "You guys worked this out together? Cool."

Mike surveyed the scene. "There's garbage rotting all over the world. This isn't even a drop in the bucket. Everyone's going to have to pitch in."

Alex eyed him skeptically. "Yeah, but you live here. If you get the garbage around here cleaned up, what do you care if there's a gigantic mess in, I don't know, Mongolia?"

Mike scowled. "Mongolia's on this planet, right? You want to live on a garbage planet?" He strode off with his shovel, and Alex had his answer.

How could a house become dirty when there weren't any occupants to mess it up? Kesha wondered as she dragged the wet mop across the kitchen floor. Somehow, a thin layer of grime had managed to deposit itself on the linoleum despite the fact that no one had walked across it for over two months. And it had to have been immaculate before the Disappearance. Her mother would never leave the house in any other condition. Even if she didn't have a choice about when she left. The last thing she needed was to come home to a dirty kitchen.

When she finished the floor, she ran around the house with a rag, in an attempt to rid the furniture of the dust that had formed on everything. She did a quick scrub of the bath and toilet, and she ran a vacuum cleaner over the carpet. She considered going up to her room. She could straighten out the mess of clothes crumpled at the bottom of her closet, the books and magazines lying all over the floor, she could even make her bed. But she decided against it. Her poor mother would already be in a state of shock when she returned. Kesha didn't want her to think her own daughter had lost her mind.

Once again, Kesha wondered if the merger had changed her at all. Shouldn't she *want* to clean up her own room now? It seemed to her that she should be feeling the effects of her own merger by now. They'd been back in New York for over twenty-four hours. She could see how others had changed. Just that morning, on the garbage landfill site, she'd noticed that Maura had grime under her fingernails. Maura, the manicure queen, with her three-inch claws. Maura, who would probably insist on her weekly nail polish when she was on her deathbed, was actually letting those precious emblems of her femininity get chipped and dirty.

The house was clean, but it still smelled musty. She opened a window in the kitchen to air out the room, and paused to listen. Someone swore he had heard a bird this morning. No one had any idea exactly how everyone would return, whether it would be a slow and gradual process or if they would all just appear as suddenly as they had disappeared. Funny, though, how none of them had any doubts that everyone *would* return, eventually.

For a brief second, she thought she could hear a dog bark, way off in the distance. But it was probably her imagination, and she wasn't about to go off in search of some stray animal. So much for caring about the universe. Maybe she was the only one who hadn't been merged at all.

She left the house, but not before checking to make sure all windows were closed and the doors were securely locked. After all, if she hadn't become a better person, a lot of other imperfect people would be returning, too, and that would include thieves.

Outside, she walked briskly. There was still plenty to do downtown at the landfill site. Plus, a group of them had planned to pick up the broken glass and other junk that lay along the streets where they'd all been hanging out. The hotel and the health club weren't in great shape either. And there was the cafeteria at Madison High—they'd torn that apart pretty well on the first night after the Disappearance. Their picky principal wasn't going to be very happy when he learned that they'd broken into all the food machines.

She cut across Central Park, and couldn't resist pausing to absorb the sensation of being alone in this enormous park. There was something magical, almost religious, about the stillness that surrounded her. She wanted to remember this. It occurred to her that she would probably—hopefully—never experience this feeling again.

On Fifth Avenue, she felt her heart jump. Blocks down the street, two figures were coming toward her, wheeling something. A baby carriage? No, it was a shopping cart. And the two figures weren't new returnees—they were Jake and Ashley.

They met at 59th Street. The shopping cart was filled with large objects loosely wrapped in brown paper.

"What's that?" Kesha asked.

"Art," Ashley told her.

"*Real* art," Jake added. "There's a Monet in there, a van Gogh, and a couple of Picassos. What you are looking at is probably around a billion dollars worth of art."

Ashley scolded him. "You should be concerned with their aesthetic value, not their value in dollars."

Jake laughed. "Yeah, well, I'll bet the Metropolitan Museum has some concern about their value in dollars."

"Is that where they came from?" Kesha asked. "You *stole* them from the Metropolitan Museum?"

"We *borrowed* them," Ashley corrected her. "They weren't any use to anyone there. At least if we brought them to the hotel, people would have a chance to see some good art."

"Yeah, people like you and Jake," Kesha said. "Where'd you keep them? In your rooms?"

Jake had the courtesy to look a little abashed. "I guess we should have put them in the lobby."

"Except they probably wouldn't have appreciated them," Ashley commented. "And some idiot like Scott or Ryan would have scribbled graffiti on them."

"You think anyone would still do that?" Kesha asked suddenly. "I mean, now that there's been this merger, would Scott behave like that?"

"I don't think this merger has turned anyone into a paragon of virtue," Jake said. "It's simply given each person something that person needed. Not everything. We're all still the same people we were. I think."

"What did *you* get?" Kesha asked.

"I think I've got more energy," Jake replied.

Kesha was disappointed. "Is that all? Your merger gave you a dose of vitamins? Besides, you've always had plenty of energy. I remember how you used to run around that track in the health club for *hours*."

"Not that kind of energy," Jake said. "It's more like . . . well, I used to daydream a lot. Now I'm ready to act on some of the dreams."

Ashley was looking around anxiously. "Jake, we'd better get moving. I'd hate to be caught outside the Metropolitan Museum with these paintings when the guards appear."

Kesha wasn't ready to let them go. "Ashley, how have you changed?" she asked urgently.

Ashley paused to consider this. "I'm not positive. But I'll tell you one thing. I'm not letting my hair grow back. I *like* it this way."

To Kesha, that didn't signify any major character change for Ashley. But Ashley wasn't finished.

"And I'm not going back to eating lettuce and carrots so I can be skinny, either."

"What about modeling?" Kesha asked. "Are you giving it up?"

"Not necessarily," Ashley said. "I'm going to start a new trend for bald models with normal bodies." She laughed. "I can't wait to see Corey's face when I tell him that."

She and Jake proceeded up Fifth while Kesha made her way down the avenue. She wished Ashley hadn't mentioned Corey. She'd been trying not to think about him. She'd asked Ashley about Corey on the plane coming home. After all, he'd been a fashion photographer and she'd been a model—there was a chance they had known each other. Still, she hadn't expected to learn that they'd been good friends.

Since returning, she'd avoided Ashley, so she wouldn't be tempted to interrogate her about the photographer. Now she wanted to run after Ashley and bombard her with a million questions.

She wondered what he looked like. What color were his eyes, how tall was he, how much did he weigh? They weren't important questions, but she couldn't help being curious. She was only human. She was *too* human. Where was that soft, flirtatious quality she thought would be hers after the merger? Why had she even thought that the merger would give her some sort of feminine delicacy?

Because that was what she had been missing. And it was becoming clear to her now that she would go on missing that quality. She was still big, aggressive, matter-of-fact Kesha Greene, with her wild messy curls, her propensity for baggy, comfortable clothes, her total inability (or desire) to wear makeup or high heels. She knew nothing about poise or grooming and had no interest in learning. She still didn't know how to flirt.

And Corey was a fashion photographer. Of all the professions in the world, why did he have a job where beauty counted more than anything else? The focus of his career was gorgeous women. His standards for good looks had to be high. The women he knew, they were the kind who had long fingernails and glossy hair, big eyes and soft skin, perfect figures. . . .

She was passing the Empire State Building. A

sudden impulse sent her inside. She knew she should be downtown, helping the others, but she couldn't resist a chance to have a few more moments alone in a special place.

She took the elevator to the top and went out onto the observation deck. She'd always loved this building, this view. What was that romantic movie where the couple vowed to meet at the top of the Empire State Building because it was the closest thing to heaven in New York? It wasn't anymore, of course. The World Trade Towers eclipsed the Empire State Building. She'd been on that observation deck too, but it wasn't the same—she didn't get the feeling of being close to heaven.

She gazed out at the city. The sun was starting to set, and the sky was pink. Which had never been one of her favorite colors, certainly not for wearing. In the sky, though, it was okay. . . .

So Jake had become more of an action person, and Ashley would gain weight. How had the others in their group changed? Shalini was talking, Alex wasn't so angry, and Travis had lost his cockiness. Cam could find romance. David could think about something *other* than romance. The merger had given each and every one of them a special gift.

But what about Kesha? Where was her gift?

The rest of the world would be coming back, changed, and she'd be the same. She'd be meeting Corey soon. Their relationship had been special. But what would he think when he saw her? What kind of expression would she see on his face? Disappointment?

Well, whatever, however he reacted, there was nothing she could do about it. She couldn't predict what he would do or say; she had no control over this. If he was turned off by her appearance, her manner, that was his problem, not hers. She was pretty sure how she'd feel: surprised to find that he wasn't the person she'd thought he was. Sad, of course, and she might hurt for a while. But she'd deal with it, she'd get over it, and she'd get on with her life. For better or worse, she was who she was and she would be who she would be, and the only person whose opinion really counted in this regard was herself.

And then she knew she had been given a gift too.

The sun had almost completely set. Lights were starting to come on all over the city. The first time Kesha had come here, she was five years old, and she was with her father. It was a Sunday, and he had promised Kesha they would go to the top of the Empire State Building that day. All day she had bugged him—"Let's go now, Daddy, can we go now?" But her father had told her that they had to go at a very special time.

They'd arrived just before sunset. Lots of other people had been up here, admiring the pink and gold scene. Little Kesha thought it was pretty too, but as the sun slowly sank, and the colors grew darker, she got bored and restless. "Is it over? Can we go down the elevator now? Can I get an ice cream?"

"Be patient, Kesha," her father had said. "It gets better. It's worth the wait."

He was right—it was. The city hadn't exploded into light—instead, the sparks of light appeared in clusters, here, there, everywhere. She recalled the way her eyes had darted around as she tried to spot every building, every window, as it lit up and cast its own little share of the glow, made its own contribution to the dazzle that was New York at night.

Just like it was doing now. Right now. For the first time in over two months. New York, the United States, the continent of North America, the Western Hemisphere, the world, was coming back to life.

She looked down and saw people. She couldn't see their faces, but she could sense their wonderment. In a facing building, she saw a hand pull back a curtain at a window. Across the street, two figures stood on a balcony. And in the glow of lights coming on all over the world, she caught glimpses of shadows, shadows of people. Billions of people who had returned to reclaim their place in the world.

Corey would be one of them. And Kesha hurried off the observation desk toward the elevator, so she, too, could get back down to earth and start looking for him.

twelve

"**good evening.** I'm Howard Chapman."

"And I'm Tammy Turner. Welcome to another edition of *One Hour*."

(*Music.*)

ANNOUNCER'S VOICE: This is *One Hour,* a weekly in-depth look at the world today, brought to you by Tingle2000, the beer of the new millennium, and Universal Airlines—"We'll get you there."

(*Commercial: "Tingle."*)

CHAPMAN: Tonight, we offer a special two-hour edition of *One Hour,* to commemorate an anniversary. It was one year ago today that humanity disappeared off the face of the Earth, only to reappear two months later, enhanced and renewed through the acceptance and absorption of an alien intelligence into our collective consciousness. Join us tonight, as *One Hour* takes a close-up look at this amazing event.

TURNER: For the next one hundred and twenty minutes, we will explore all the ramifications and consequences of this unprecedented occurrence. In retrospect, we ask: where are we as a race and as individuals? How have we changed? What have we gained? What, if anything, have we lost?

CHAPMAN: And what about the personalities who emerged in the crisis? The teens who were left behind on Earth—where are they now? The ten who claimed responsibility for the rescue of mankind—should they be considered heroes? Or did they sell us out?

TURNER: All these questions, and more, will be addressed in this special edition of *One Hour*. Stay with us!

(*Commercial: "Share a Tingle with a Friend."*)

CHAPMAN: I sincerely doubt that there are any viewers tonight who don't remember asking themselves this question ten months ago, when we found ourselves back in our bodies, unsure if we'd ever been away. (*Holds up issue of* USA Today *with headline: What Happened?*) While we were all grateful to find ourselves back on Earth, we were in a state of total confusion. Do you remember where you were, Tammy, and how you felt?

TURNER: I certainly do, Howard. I was in California at the time of the Disappearance, on vacation, and like many people on vacation, I was sleeping late. When I returned to Earth, I thought I'd just had a rather lengthy and bizarre dream!

CHAPMAN (*Chuckles*): I know what you mean, Tammy. I myself was en route to cover a demonstration in midtown at the time of the Disappearance, early afternoon. When I returned, my first thought was that we had been in an accident and we were all dead. Imagine my reaction when

I looked out the window and saw that I was on Forty-second Street and Broadway. I hadn't expected heaven to look like Times Square at dusk, with hordes of New Yorkers and tourists wandering around looking completely stunned!

TURNER: Did it occur to you that you might have gone to the other place? (*Laughs.*) But seriously, Howard, we were all left with a lot of questions. Of course, there were those who refused to believe that anything had happened, that it was all some sort of dream. To this day, there is an organized group that claims the whole event was nothing more than a government conspiracy to control the world's population. There were claims that the so-called alien consciousness within us is actually an implant that reads our minds. But in the days just following the reappearance of people on Earth, reactions were many and varied.

(*Clip: ordinary man on the street.*)

MAN: We were abducted by aliens! They ate our brains! I have proof!

TURNER: For once, we couldn't dismiss this type of reaction as groundless hysteria. In the days following the Return, witnesses came forward and confirmed that what had seemed like a nightmare to many had, in fact, occurred. One of the first to come forward was Maura Kelly, one of the high school students in New York City that stayed on Earth during the Disappearance.

(*Clip: Maura Kelly.*)

MAURA: At first, we thought everyone else was gone for good. But we had a feeling that people still existed, somewhere, and we didn't give up hope. We were all working hard at trying to make contact. Except for David Chu—all he wanted to do was party. Anyway, some of us stayed in New York, and some of us went to California. Because, like, we didn't know where the aliens would make contact. I mean, they could have beamed up the ones who stayed in New York. It was just dumb luck that the California group was chosen. But I guess you could say that all of us pretty much saved the world.

CHAPMAN (*Smiles*): Ah, the arrogance of youth. But twenty-five students from New York's Madison High School did find themselves alone on Earth, and ten of them actually claim to have negotiated the Return with the aliens. Tonight, one of those teenagers joins us by satellite from our sister station in Portland, Oregon.

(*Cut to Portland studio.*)

CHAPMAN: Martina, thank you for joining us. Now, you were among the ten Madison High students who take the credit for the survival of humanity. Is that correct?

MARTINA: Well, not me personally. But we were the ones who were actually communicating with them. The rest of the world was just—there. Somewhere. We couldn't see them or talk to them.

CHAPMAN: Looking back now, what can you tell us about the experience?

MARTINA: It was pretty weird. The aliens were like one consciousness. They didn't have bodies, and they couldn't feel anything. At first, they just wanted to inhabit our bodies and experience sensations. But we finally reached an agreement so they could merge with us, and we could all live together.

TURNER: Martina, tell our viewers—did your group ever consider other options?

MARTINA: Like what?

TURNER: Well, what about going on the offensive, fighting the alien spirit instead of automatically going for a compromise solution?

MARTINA: There was one member of our group, Alex Popov, who thought we should fight them. But there were only ten of us! And how could we fight them if we couldn't even see them? And what if we lost?

TURNER: And how do you respond to your critics, like Senator T. Hudson Darrow, who have stated publicly that you and your friends should be censored, or even indicted, as traitors to the human race?

MARTINA: Well, he wasn't there. I suggest he talk to his son Travis.

TURNER: Which brings us to the personal impact of the event. Later, we will be talking with young Travis Darrow, son of the outspoken senator. But right now, tell us, Martina, how has the experience affected you on a personal level?

MARTINA: Um, well, I don't know, really. . . .

TURNER: You were supposedly one of the first to believe that humanity continued to exist after the Disappearance. This had something to do with the fact that you're an identical twin, and your twin sister, Rosa, was abducted along with the rest of the human race. Am I correct?

MARTINA: Yes . . .

TURNER: How is your relationship with your sister

now? Is she grateful to you for having rescued her?

MARTINA: I don't know. We're not really that close anymore. I think that once we merged with the spirit, it helped us to develop our own individualities, and so . . .

TURNER: Is it possible that perhaps Rosa resents the fact that you allowed her to merge with an alien spirit without asking her permission?

MARTINA: But that's not how it happened!

TURNER: How did it happen, Martina?

MARTINA: I don't know. It's just—happened.

(*Close-up on Turner.*)

TURNER: It just happened, she says. Perhaps that's all we'll ever know. Eyewitness accounts have been, to say the least, contradictory. For now, we'll put aside how this happened and ask ourselves, what are the consequences?

(*Commercial: "Tingle: the Ultimate Sensation."*)

CHAPMAN: Welcome back. We're privileged to have with us today the first internationally elected official of the new World Legislature, former United States Senator T. Hudson Darrow. Mr. Darrow, what can you tell us about the effect of the alien merger on our global society?

DARROW: To begin with, I prefer to use the phrase "the alleged merger," since there is no scientific proof of a merger.

CHAPMAN: Fine. What can you tell us about the effect of the alleged alien merger on our global society?

DARROW: It is clearly apparent that in the past ten months there has been surprisingly accelerated progress in a number of areas. For example, peace initiatives in the Middle East, Northern Ireland, the former Yugoslavia, the former Soviet Union, and the former European Community are moving forward. The international economic structure has stabilized, and there are ongoing efforts to organize aid to nations that are threatened by famine, disease, and national disaster.

CHAPMAN: That sounds like we're doing pretty well to me.

DARROW: That may be a premature assumption. We have not yet completed research in the area of possible negative consequences.

CHAPMAN: Senator, your own son was one of the original young people who made contact with the alien society. You have been quoted as saying that your son is not the same, that his personality appears to be altered. Would you comment on that?

DARROW: I would rather not. My family situation is not relevant to this conversation.

CHAPMAN: Then what about the environment? Could you comment on that?

DARROW: This is not under my jurisdiction. I will ask my colleague Dr. Berger to respond to that question. He's an environmental specialist.

CHAPMAN: Well, it looks like this merger—excuse me, alleged merger—hasn't had any impact on the nature of bureaucracy! Good evening, Dr. Berger.

BERGER: Good evening.

CHAPMAN: What can you tell us about the environment?

BERGER: Great strides are being taken to ensure that what our alien friends tell us happened to their original world will not happen to ours. As a result of recent drastic pollution controls, the air is cleaner now than it was a century ago. New initiatives include a recycling plan which raises garbage separation to an art form. Of course, the success of this plan will depend on cooperation at the local level.

CHAPMAN: And to comment on local consequences, we go to correspondent George Clark, who is with the mayor of New York City. George?

CLARK: Thank you, Howard. I am pleased to be standing here with the honorable mayor of the great city of New York. Mr. Mayor, what can you tell us about New York today as compared to a year ago?

MAYOR: Crime is down. Drug abuse is down. Subways are running on time, the streets are clean, and New York taxi drivers are more courteous than ever. The quality of life in this city has improved enormously. However, I'm not sure how much of this improvement is due to the merger. I'd like to think that my administration has had some impact. Certainly, I cannot give credit to the adolescents who wreaked havoc in the fair city for two months. The Washington Square landfill, for example, was executed in an amateur fashion, and it was thoughtless and immature of those young people to utilize prime Manhattan real estate for this purpose. Our retail stores are still attempting to recoup merchandise stolen during the Disappearance, and the Metropolitan Museum of Art suspects that certain priceless works of art were actually handled by these teenage hooligans.

CHAPMAN: And what about the quality of life out-side the United States? After this message, we'll hear from our Paris correspondent, Christine Far-rell.

(*Commercial: "Everybody wants to Tingle."*)

FARRELL: Hello, Tammy, Howard. I'm standing here by the Eiffel Tower, the symbol of the city that prides itself on its growing reputation as the friendliest place in Europe. And with me are two young people whose direct encounter with the alien life-form has led to a dramatic change in their lives. One year ago, Travis Darrow was planning to follow in his esteemed father's foot-steps—first, to St. John's University, then on to Harvard Law School, and finally emerging to take his place in the political world in which his father and grandfather have played a notable role. In *Time* magazine profile of his family two years ago, the senator described his son as a leader of tomorrow. Travis, what are you doing today?

TRAVIS: (*unintelligible*).

FARRELL: I'm sorry, Travis, I didn't catch that.

DONNA: We're just hanging out.

(*Camera pans back to include his female compan-ion in picture.*)

FARRELL: And you are—

DONNA: I'm Donna Caparelli. I was there, too.

FARRELL: Yes, of course. Now, Travis, your father tells us that the experience caused a significant alteration in your personality. In essence, he says that you are no longer the son he knew. What do you say to that?

TRAVIS: (*unintelligible*).

DONNA: His father never knew him. Travis didn't know himself. The alien spirit released him from the role he was playing, and he's now discovering who he really is. I'm learning a lot about myself, too. Me and Travis, we're just roaming the world, enjoying all the new sensations.

FARRELL: Can you speak for yourself, Travis?

DONNA: Not really. He's very shy.

FARRELL: Can you tell us something about your plans for the future?

DONNA: We're just going to hang out for a while. Find ourselves, you know? Because we're not the same people we were before. None of us are.

FARRELL: And that goes for you too, Travis?

TRAVIS: (*Close-up*):Yeah.

FARRELL: (*Looks at camera, shrugs, sad what-can-you-do smile*): Back to you in New York, Howard.

CHAPMAN: Thank you, Christine.

TURNER: I don't know about you, Howard, but when I see that face, "leader" isn't the word that comes to my mind.

CHAPMAN: I know what you mean, Tammy. But there are those for whom the experience has brought a change in values. For example, volunteerism has been increasing at a remarkable rate in recent months. Joining us here in the studio is David Chu, another of the twenty-five young people we mentioned earlier. He is on his way to join one of the international aid camps that have been set up around the world. Thank you for joining us, David.

DAVID: Glad to be here.

CHAPMAN: David, one of your classmates, Maura

Kelly, implied that you weren't very interested in saving the world last year at this time. And yet now you're on your way to join thousands of volunteers in helping impoverished communities around the world. Would you say that this change in your attitude resulted from the alien merger?

DAVID: I don't know.

CHAPMAN: Well, do you know what you'll be doing as a volunteer?

DAVID: Some kind of physical labor, I think. Help build houses, plant stuff—whatever they tell me to do.

CHAPMAN: That certainly sounds admirable. What made you decide to join in the volunteer effort?

DAVID: I've heard that a lot of girls are joining these camps. And the atmosphere is pretty loose, y'know? Sort of like a Club Med, only you can't lie on the beach all day. Anyway, there's this camp in Mexico that's supposed to be a nonstop party.

CHAPMAN: I see. Thank you, David.

TURNER: Well, it doesn't sound to me like that young man has had a major personality overhaul! But another of the young people from that group has certainly found direction. We go now to Rome, where correspondent Rodney Benson is with supermodel Ashley Silver. Rodney?

BENSON: Thank you, Howard. A year ago, Ashley Silver was just another baby model, one of a thousand of thin teenage girls who subsist on lettuce leaves for the privilege of appearing in the pages of fashion magazines or strutting the runways in Paris, New York, and Milan. Today, she is a star.

(*Clip: Ashley Silver prancing down a runway that is lined with cheering throngs and flashing lights. Cut to Benson with Silver.*)

BENSON: Tell me, Ashley, in your opinion, before the Disappearance and the merger, could a bald, two-hundred-pound young woman have become a supermodel?

SILVER: Oh, sure.

BENSON: (*Surprised*): Do you really believe that?

SILVER: I think we've always known that beauty comes in all shapes and sizes, but we were such chickens, we let the fashion industry tell us how we should look. But when you start really caring about other people, you stop judging them by artificially imposed standards. The alien spirit knew that. And we knew that, too. We just didn't have the guts to act on it. Take my boyfriend, Jake, for example. He thought he fell in love with me because I was considered beautiful. Now, he realizes he loves me for reasons that have nothing to do with how I look. And he thinks I'm even more beautiful today.

BENSON: Would you say we should be thankful for the alien merger?

SILVER: Absolutely. They saved us.

BENSON: Back to you, Howard.

CHAPMAN: It sounds like Ashley is saying the alien spirit is the real hero. What do you think about that, Tammy?

TURNER: (*Smiles*). She's eighteen, Howard. (*Turns to camera.*) We'll be back in a moment.

(*Commercial: "Universal Airlines: The World Is Your Home."*)

TURNER: The merger has certainly had a significant impact on art, literature, music, and theater. But whether the impact has been positive is a matter of dispute. Statistics tell us that people are reading more, that art galleries and museums have had more visitors in the past ten months than in the past ten years. Film and theater attendance is at an all-time high. On the other hand, critics tell us that what passes for art now is dull and derivative. At the opening of a photography exhibit in New York, I spoke to Kesha Greene, another of the Madison High group.

(*Clip: Turner and Greene.*)

TURNER: Kesha, an art critic called this exhibition boring. What is your opinion of this show?

KESHA: I think it's fantastic. Look at these portraits of people before and after the merger.

TURNER: They look the same.

KESHA: Exactly! We haven't changed. We're just more receptive. And nobody cares what critics say anymore. All that matters is what the people think. And they think it's great. A photographer like Corey is now free to express himself without worrying about what some snotty old creep will say about his work.

TURNER: But what about standards? Without critics, how will art be evaluated?

KESHA: By the people who experience it. Who needs critics to impose their opinions on us? We don't judge people by artificially imposed standards anymore. Why should we judge art? It's hard to believe that there was a time when women faced discrimination because of their sex, or when racial inequality was rampant. Today, as a Black woman, I am considered to have no less significance in the world than a white man. And if we're not going to judge people by how they look, why should we judge art? Or movies, or books, or music, or—

TURNER: Yes, we get your point, Kesha. Thank you.

CHAPMAN: That was an interesting observation, Tammy.

TURNER: Yes, but I think we'd should keep in mind the fact that Kesha is currently involved in a relationship with this particular photographer. She may not be the most objective critic of his work! And speaking of critics, no one seems to be very happy with the sports world these days.

CHAPMAN: That's right, Tammy, and it's a cause of concern for coaches, players, and their fans. No one was surprised when last winter's basketball season was a little slow. We blamed that on general disorientation after the merger. But the baseball season was a washout too, with lackadaisical play. Now we're in the football season, and things aren't looking too good. It's as if the players are too busy looking out for each other to compete. For thoughts on this, let's hear from network sports announcer Mel Baron. Mel?

BARON: Well, Howard, no one knows what's going on. Some believe that the merger has sapped the strength of athletes. Others believe that we're entering an unprecedented era of good sportsmanship. The general attitude among players seems to be the old adage, "It doesn't matter whether you win or lose, it's how you play the game." But in the long run, it all comes down to the same thing. From soccer to ice hockey, sports have become boring. The athletes have lost interest in competing. I talked to the coach of the Dallas Cowboys about this the other day, and here's what he had to say.

(*Clip: Baron and coach in football stadium.*)

COACH: Well, I can guarantee you, Mel, the Cowboys aren't going to turn into little prissy proper gentlemen athlete wimps. There's too much at stake. It's going to be a long, hard road, but we're going to make our boys mean again.

BARON: So, the world of sports may have a future after all, Howard.

CHAPMAN: That's good news, Mel. And there's more good news coming from the world of technology. I spoke to Cameron Daley, one of the young people from Madison High, who now, despite his youth, is a consultant at Foley Laboratories.

(*Clip: Chapman with Daley in laboratory.*)

CHAPMAN: Cameron, you've been asked by Foley Laboratories to lend your personal experience with the aliens to their research into new modes of communication. This must be quite a thrill for an eighteen-year-old boy. What kind of work are you doing?

DALEY: I'm conducting a series of tests in the area of nonverbal connections, based on the interpretation of brain waves. Our ultimate goal is to identify a form of communication which will eliminate the need for human contact. Just as telephones freed us to speak without being in close physical contact, a reliable form of telepathic communication would mean we wouldn't even have to speak to each other.

CHAPMAN: (*Smiles*): But some of us like having human contact, Cameron.

DALEY: Yeah, sure, but wouldn't it be nice to choose? For example, I like having human contact with my girlfriend, but with the ability to make a nonverbal connection, you and I could be having this interview, and I wouldn't even have to meet you.

TURNER: Well, Howard, it doesn't look like the alien encounter or the merger has improved the manners of teenagers.

CHAPMAN: That's the truth, Tammy. And there are other aspects of adolescence that haven't changed. Take a look at Alex Popov, another Madison High student.

(*Clip: small group of university students.*)

POPOV: We're individuals, and they can't take that away from us! We have the right to express our feelings! Anger is good! We don't have to get along with everybody. We can compete, we can fight, we can hate our neighbors. Be yourself— don't let the military-industrial-entertainment complex run your life!

TURNER: Popov has been the most outspoken of the Madison High group. He travels to schools and university campuses and talks to young people about the dangers of being too satisfied. But his efforts to stir up discontent haven't been particularly successful. To get some insight into this unusual character, I spoke to his ex-girlfriend, Shalini Chatterjee.

(*Clip: Turner with Chatterjee.*)

TURNER: Shalini, why does Alex feel the need to find fault with the merger?

SHALINI: Because he's Alex, and he finds fault with everything.

TURNER: Then the merger didn't improve his nature?

SHALINI: On the contrary! He used to keep all his anger and bitterness inside. Now he expresses it.

TURNER: And what about you, Shalini? What has the merger offered you?

SHALINI: It gave me the strength to break off a relationship that was too lopsided. And the strength to be myself.

CHAPMAN: It's ironic, isn't it, Tammy. According to Shalini, it took the absorption of another entity to give us the courage to be ourselves. And yet, can we be sure that all humans everywhere, have experienced a merger with the alien consciousness. (*Turns to camera.*) We'll be back with some final thoughts in a moment.

(*Commercial: new fall program previews—Alien Medical Center, My Alien Neighbors, I Married an Alien.*)

CHAPMAN: What has this retrospective told us about the state of the world today? Are we in better shape than we were before? Or have we lost more than we gained? Only time will tell. Next week will see the release of *What Really Happened* by Jake Robbins. Robbins, one of the young people who actually met the alien consciousness before the merger, has written what he claims to be the only true account of the disappearance of humanity, the convergence with aliens, and the return of humanity merged with an alien consciousness. The book is not without controversy. Early reports from critics state that much of the work is pure fiction, that there are major discrepancies between earlier reports from the young people and Robbins's recollections. I caught up with Robbins last week and asked him about this.

(*Clip: Chapman and Robbins.*)

CHAPMAN: How do you respond to critics who say that your account contradicts other reports from your group?

ROBBINS: Maybe I needed time to recover the memories.

CHAPMAN: But is it possible that the passage of time has erased some memories?

ROBBINS: Maybe. I guess we'll never know, will we?

TURNER: And that just about sums it up, doesn't it? We'll never really know what happened. And does that matter anyway?

CHAPMAN: Thank you for joining us tonight. And be with us next week, when *One Hour* will look at recently uncovered evidence that casts a new light on the assassination of John F. Kennedy. Could an alien conspiracy have initiated the tragic events of November 22, 1963? Good night, and have a good week.

Thought-Provoking Novels
from Today's Headlines

HOMETOWN
by Marsha Qualey   72921-0/$3.99 US/$4.99 Can
Border Baker isn't happy about moving to his father's rural
Minnesota hometown, where they haven't forgotten that
Border's father fled to Canada rather than serve in Vietnam.
Now, as a new generation is bound for the Persian Gulf, the
town wonders about the son of a draft dodger.

NOTHING BUT THE TRUTH
by Avi   71907-X/$4.99 US /$6.99 Can
Philip was just humming along with *The Star Spangled
Banner*, played each day in his homeroom. How could this
minor incident turn into a major national scandal?

TWELVE DAYS IN AUGUST
by Liza Ketchum Murrow   72353-0/$3.99 US/$4.99 Can
Sixteen-year-old Todd is instantly attracted to Rita Beckman,
newly arrived in Todd's town from Los Angeles. But when
Todd's soccer teammate Randy starts spreading the rumor that
Rita's twin brother Alex is gay, Todd isn't sure he has the
courage to stick up for Alex.

THE HATE CRIME
by Phyllis Karas   78214-6/$3.99 US/$4.99 Can
Zack's dad is the district attorney, so Zack hears about all
kinds of terrible crimes. The latest case is about graffiti defac-
ing the local temple. But it's only when Zack tries to get to the
bottom of this senseless act that he fully understands the terror
these vicious scrawls evoke.

Award-winning author
NORMA FOX MAZER

MISSING PIECES
72289-5/$4.50 US/$5.99 Can

Jessie's father walked out on his family when she was just a baby. Why should she care about him—it's clear he never cared about her. Yet after years of anxiety, a determined Jessie needs to know more about him, and over her mother's objections, Jessie decides to track him down.

DOWNTOWN
88534-4/$4.50 US/$5.99 Can

Sixteen-year-old Pete Greenwood is the son of fugitive radicals of the 1960's. Pete has been telling everyone that his parents are dead because it was easier than telling the truth. But when Pete meets Cary, someone he can really talk to, he wonders if he can trust her with his terrible secret.

And Don't Miss

OUT OF CONTROL   71347-0/$4.50 US/$5.99 Can
BABYFACE   75720-6/$4.99 US/$6.99 Can
SILVER   75026-0/$4.99 US/$6.50 Can
AFTER THE RAIN   75025-2/$4.50 US/$5.99 Can
TAKING TERRI MUELLER   79004-1/$4.50 US/$5.99 Can